P9-DXZ-465

1/22

Meena

LOST
AND FOUND

Also by Karla Manternach

Meena Meets Her Match
Never Fear, Meena's Here!

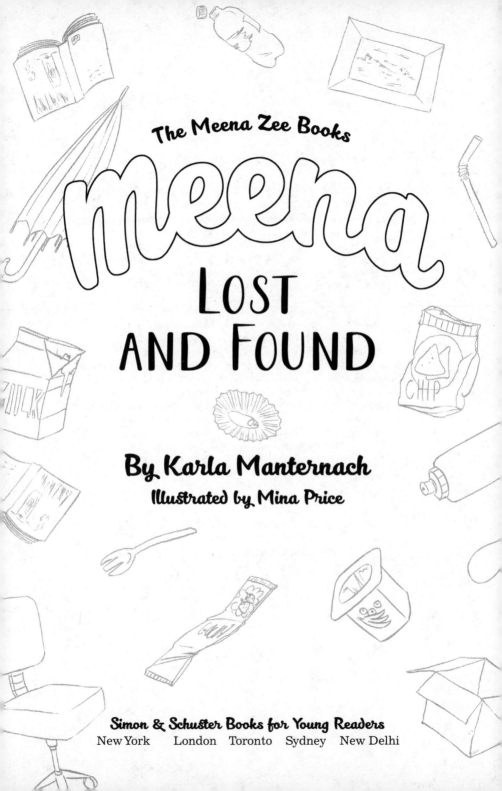

The Meena Zee Books

meena
LOST
AND FOUND

By Karla Manternach
Illustrated by Mina Price

Simon & Schuster Books for Young Readers
New York   London   Toronto   Sydney   New Delhi

SIMON & SCHUSTER BOOKS FOR YOUNG READERS
An imprint of Simon & Schuster Children's Publishing Division
1230 Avenue of the Americas, New York, New York 10020
This book is a work of fiction. Any references to historical events,
real people, or real places are used fictitiously. Other names, characters, places,
and events are products of the author's imagination, and any resemblance to actual
events or places or persons, living or dead, is entirely coincidental.
Text © 2021 by Karla Manternach
Illustrations © 2021 by Mina Price
All rights reserved, including the right of reproduction in whole or in part in any form.
SIMON & SCHUSTER BOOKS FOR YOUNG READERS
and related marks are trademarks of Simon & Schuster, Inc.
For information about special discounts for bulk purchases, please contact Simon &
Schuster Special Sales at 1-866-506-1949 or business@simonandschuster.com.
The Simon & Schuster Speakers Bureau can bring authors to your live event.
For more information or to book an event, contact the Simon & Schuster Speakers Bureau
at 1-866-248-3049 or visit our website at www.simonspeakers.com.
Book design by Tom Daly
The text for this book was set in Excelsior LT.
The illustrations for this book were rendered digitally
Manufactured in the United States of America
0921 FFG
First Edition
2 4 6 8 10 9 7 5 3 1
CIP data for this book is available from the Library of Congress.
ISBN 9781534486140
ISBN 9781534486164 (eBook)

For Brian, Amelia, and Mara—
I'd be lost without you

Our milk jug igloo is the perfect spot for club meetings.

I drop to my knees and crawl inside. It's cool and wet today, but it's cozy and dry in here. Milk lids dot the walls in rainbow colors—blue for skim, green for low fat, and red for whole. We even have orange, which you can only get if you buy those milk jugs full of juice!

The only color that's missing is pink for strawberry milk. I feel a twinge in my stomach every time I notice. Sofía would have brought those jugs, but we were in a fight when we built the igloo, so I didn't invite her.

At least she's part of the club now. I call through the doorway, "Are you two coming?"

My cousin Eli crawls in and sits across from me, his muddy knees the same color as his freckles. "She's checking for eggs again," he says with a grin.

I groan. Eli's chicken coop is on the back

porch too, and Sofía can't stay away from it. She's always watching the chickens peck at their feathers or opening the little drawers to look for eggs. I'm about to call her again when I stop.

Give her a minute, I tell myself.

I've been Sofía's best friend since kindergarten, but . . . well, I haven't always been very good at it. Sometimes I forget to give her a turn or listen to her ideas. A few times I've stopped talking to her because I was mad or hurt. I *do* listen when she moans about getting a word wrong on her spelling test. I put up with the way she smooths out the blankets after I sit on her bed. She also has a thing about wearing black socks with her blue sneakers, and I've never once said anything about it.

But Sofía has been a much better friend to me. She helps me collect beautiful trash. She trades lunch food with me to make sure I get every color of the rainbow. And this year, when I started having seizures, and none of the other kids would come near me, Sofía stayed right by my side.

I spin the friendship bracelet around my wrist and make myself wait. It's her club too, even if it *is* my turn to be president.

When she finally crawls in, I scooch back against the wall, pick up our big metal spoon, and clang it against the floor. "Order! Order! The Finders Keepers Club is now in session! Vice President Eli, what's first on our agenda?"

"Snacks. I brought popcorn." He rattles the bag in his hand and empties it onto the floorboards in the middle of our circle.

"I brought *chicles*," Sofía says, reaching into her pocket. The little rectangles click as she drops them into the pile. Technically, they aren't a snack, since you aren't supposed to swallow gum, but they come in cool flavors like cough drop and black jelly bean.

I reach into the front pocket of my tie-dyed hoodie. "I brought animal crackers." I open the little box, dump it onto the floor, and scoop up a handful.

"Next is savings," Eli says.

I crunch on my snack and turn to Sofía. "Madam Treasurer, how much money have we found?"

She peeks inside the spare jug we use for a bank. "Nine cents since we started the club. Four pennies and a nickel."

We nod at each other, impressed. Eli was the one who spotted the nickel two weeks ago, but I found three of the pennies myself, which is the most *coins*, even if it isn't worth the most.

Not that it's a contest or anything.

I swallow and pick up two cinnamon *chicles*. My mouth turns spicy as I chew.

"Treasures next," Eli says. "I'll go first." He opens the little baggie in his lap and holds up a limp yellow leaf.

"It looks like a fan," Sofía says.

"That's because it's from a gingko tree." He passes it around then holds up an acorn.

"What's so great about that?" I ask. "They're all over the place."

"But the top of this one is still attached," he says. "Usually they come apart before you find them."

I nod. "Okay, cool. What's your third thing?"

He reaches into his bag again and pulls out a pinecone. Only when I look closer, I see that it's actually a *double* pinecone, fused together like a monster with two heads!

"Nice," Sofía says, tracing it with her finger.

"Your turn," he says to her when we've both had a chance to look. "What'd you find this week?"

Sofía lights up and opens her worn-out bird book. She doesn't like finding treasures the way Eli and I do, but she's always looking for the birds that are listed in her book, so we decided that could count as her collection. "I saw a blue jay this morning," she says, holding up a picture.

I try to seem excited, but I'm not gonna lie. I was kind of hoping for an ostrich.

"What was it doing?" Eli asks sharply.

Sofía blinks. "Just sitting there."

He crosses his arms. "Blue jays are mean, you know. They attack other birds."

"They're so pretty, though." She fingers the edge of the page. "Their tail feathers look like stained-glass windows."

Eli's face softens. "What else did you see?"

"A lot more robins this week," she says, turning pages. "And I didn't see it, but I heard a red-winged blackbird."

"I saw a junco yesterday," Eli says.

"Really?"

"The squirrels scared him off, though. They haven't gotten into my feeder, but they chase away the birds that eat from the ground." He brightens. "Wanna hear me do a squirrel?"

Oh, no. If Eli gets started with his sound effects, I might never get a turn. He stretches his mouth wide and makes a scratchy sound in the back of this throat. *"Ack-ack-ack!"*

Sofía beams at him. "You sound just like one!"

Eli smiles, his ears going pink.

I sigh and start twisting the strings of my hoodie.

I think Sofía notices, though, because she bumps her shoulder against mine and says, "What did you find this week?"

Finally!

I sit up straighter. Not to brag, but I'd say my trash collection is the highlight of our meetings. I reach into my pocket and pull out a scraped-up doll head with rainbow streaks in her hair. "I found this in a parking lot," I say, "but I added the highlights myself. And check this out!" I open my hand to show them an oval sunglass lens that looks like a mirror. Last but not least, I pull out my favorite find of the week: a red plastic comb with so many missing teeth that—

"It looks like the letter E!" Sofía says.

I hand it to Eli. "Just two more letters, and I'll be able to write your name in trash."

He laughs.

"I have something else for the agenda too," I say.

He passes the comb to Sofía. "What?"

"Our club needs a project."

Sofía tilts her head at me. "We already have a project. We collect treasures."

"But we need something else. Something bigger. I was thinking . . ." I lean in closer. "You know how you see some stores and restaurants all over, no matter how far you go from home?"

They nod.

"I think our club should be like that."

"Like a chain?" Eli asks.

"Why not?" I ask. "This would still be our main headquarters, but we could open clubhouses all over town—all over the world, even. And when people land on Mars, we could be the first kids in the whole human race to build a clubhouse there!"

Eli raises his eyebrows at me. "You want to expand to other planets?"

"We can start with a new location in town."

"Where?" Sofía asks.

"At your place." I loop my pinky through her friendship bracelet. "You should get the next clubhouse since you didn't get to help build this one. All those in favor?" I put my hand in the air.

They shrug at each other and raise their hands.

"Yes!" I'm so happy that I throw my arms out, lean back against the wall, and—

Oh! I'm falling!

The jugs squeak as the wall shifts behind me. Sofía grabs my arm and pulls me up as the roof caves in. "Don't let it break," I cry, pushing against the dome. Eli and Sofía use their hands to brace the jugs in place.

The squeaking stops. I hold my breath. We stare at one another with big eyes.

"What do we do?" Sofía asks.

Slowly, I ease my hands away. The ceiling sags a little more. "Wait here," I say, scrambling out the door.

In a minute, I crawl back in with an umbrella from the hall closet.

"What are you gonna do with that?" Eli asks.

"Open it. But I don't want it to smack you in the face. On the count of three, you hit the floor. Ready? One, two, three!"

Eli and Sofía duck. I press the release. The ceiling starts to droop, but the umbrella opens, catches it, and lifts it away from us.

We all let out a big breath.

"That was close," I say. It looks like a circus tent in here now with the striped umbrella above us.

"But you can't hold it forever," Sofía says.

"I'll get something to prop it up," Eli says. He scurries out and comes back with a big white bucket.

He sets it in the middle of the igloo, and I carefully rest the handle of the umbrella on the lid. When I'm pretty sure it's steady, I let go. The umbrella tips a little, but it stays balanced on the bucket and holds up the dome. We crawl out to check for damage.

The igloo is lopsided now, and the wall has a big bulge where I fell against it. But at least it's still in one piece. I grin at them. "Good as new!"

Eli stares at me. "Are you serious?"

"Yeah! If you tilt your head, you can't even tell how crooked it is. Try it."

He does, but he still says, "I don't think that'll last."

"Sure it will."

There's a gust of wind, and the dome of jugs sways. I jump forward and throw out my arms, like maybe hugging the whole igloo would help. The wind dies down and the igloo goes still again.

I cringe. "It'll be okay, right?"

Eli and Sofía glance at each other.

I give the igloo a worried look. "Why don't we—"

Ack-ack-ack!

Eli holds up a hand. "Shhh," he says, turning toward the yard.

Sofía and I freeze. For a minute, I don't hear anything except the soft clucking of the chickens in the coop behind us. Then the sound comes again.

Ack-ack-ack!

"A squirrel!" Eli clambers down the porch steps with a loud bellow, waving his arms over his head. Sofía and I chase after him in time to see birds scattering into the air and something zipping away from the feeder. Sofía gasps as it streaks through the yard and disappears into the brush.

"What was that?" I ask. It didn't look like a squirrel. It was white with colored spots.

"I don't know," Eli says. "Maybe a rabbit?"

Sofía starts moving toward the brush and stops.

I trail after her. "What's the matter?" I ask, following her gaze. "What are you looking at?"

"That wasn't a rabbit," she says. She turns to us then, her eyes wide. "I think it was Oriol."

Oriol?" I ask. "What would he be doing here?"

Sofía hurries toward the brush and starts calling him in a singsong. "Oriol! Oriol!"

We fan out to look. Eli makes a clicking sound with his mouth. I try calling, "Here, kitty, kitty!" Sofía's cat has never come to me before, and I don't know why he'd start now, but I feel like I should do *something* to help.

After a few minutes, we still haven't found him. "Are you sure it was him?" Eli asks. "I've never seen him here before."

"Maybe not," Sofía says. She sounds doubtful.

"Even if it was," I say, "he's probably on his way back home."

I don't see what the big deal is. Oriol is always wandering around Sofía's yard. Who cares if he's gone a few blocks farther?

I glance back at the porch. "We should check on the igloo," I say. "Maybe we could fill it up with balloons so it won't collapse. Or we could build some kind of frame for it inside, like a skeleton. Or what if we hung something from the porch ceiling to hold it up?"

Nobody answers.

I shift from one foot to the other. It took months to pull enough jugs out of the neighborhood recycling bins to build our igloo. And it was worth it! It turned out even better than I imagined! We can't let anything happen to it now.

But Sofía just keeps squinting into the brush. She almost always goes along with whatever I want. For a long time, I figured it was because I have the best ideas.

Now I think sometimes I forget to ask what *she* wants.

I guess the igloo will be okay for a while. I hope.

"Would you rather go to your house?" I ask. "Make sure Oriol is there?"

Sofía looks at me. "You don't mind?"

I stuff my hands into my front pocket and cross my fingers. Technically, I'm about to tell a tiny lie, and I don't want it to count. "I don't mind."

She takes a big breath and nods.

I reach under my hoodie, unclip the walkie-talkie from the waistband of my pants, and press the talk button. "Big Zee to Zee Money. Come in, Zee Money, over."

There's a pause, then my dad's voice crackles

through the speaker. "Zee Money here. Go ahead, over."

"Zookeeper and I are headed to the Flamingo's. Do you copy, over?"

"I copy, Big Zee. Stick together, and holler when you get there, over."

"Roger that, Zee Money. Over and out."

I hook the walkie-talkie back onto my pants. I get to go a lot more places on my own since I started using it. I got the idea from those CB radio things that truck drivers use in old movies. Mom and Dad won't let me have my own phone, but at least this makes me feel like a trucker!

Eli calls through the back door to tell Aunt Kathy where we're going, then we pocket our treasures and head for Sofía's. The world's a lot more colorful now that it's spring. The grass is turning green, and the tulips are blooming—red and purple and yellow. It rained this morning, and it's still cold enough that I pull the sleeves of my sweatshirt over my hands as we walk.

Eli runs ahead to rescue earthworms that are stranded on the sidewalk. Sofía trails behind, looking for birds. I stoop to pick up a worm that Eli missed then check the curb for interesting trash.

I find most of my treasures after the garbage truck comes by on Wednesdays. It has mechanical arms that lift the bins to dump them into the back.

Sometimes the wind catches little bits of trash as they're falling. It sends them flying around the streets until somebody picks them up again.

Usually that somebody is me. I'm not exactly a tidy-up-after-myself kind of a kid, but I do keep this neighborhood pretty clean.

We're still a few houses from Sofía's when I stop.

Someone put a *ton* of cool stuff on the curb. It's a trash jackpot! There's a big flowerpot with a crack in it, a rake with a broken handle, and a lawn chair that's turned inside out. There's even a rusty old wagon. It's all just sitting here with a sign that says *free*, the best word in the world.

"Look at this," I say when Sofía catches up to me. "Why are people getting rid of so much great stuff lately?"

She shrugs. "Spring cleaning?"

I give her a funny look. Why would anybody clean when it's finally nice outside? Or ever?

I turn back to the wonderful pile of trash. If I had a pickup truck, I'd take it *all*. I could drive around every month on bulk trash day, talking to other truckers on my CB radio and hauling away the cool stuff people chuck onto the curb.

Hang on.

My eyes zoom in on the wagon. The metal bottom is flaky with rust, and when I pull it out of the

pile, one of the wheels screeches. But it's big enough for me to load up the whole pile of trash. It's all mine now!

"What are you gonna do with that?" Sofía asks as I haul my wagon down the sidewalk.

"Something *awesome*." My brain sparks with ideas. "Maybe we'll use it for our new clubhouse!"

She looks at me. "Don't you want to build it out of milk jugs?"

"We can use whatever we want. Every location can be one of a kind!" I get a zillion Inspirations thinking about it—walls made of lawn chair webbing, pillars made of old garden tools, upside-down flowerpots turned into seats!

Then I catch myself. Sofía should get to pick. We don't exactly have the same style. When she showed me how to make *cascarones* for Easter, her confetti eggs turned out pretty and pastel. Mine were covered in so many little globs of tissue paper that they were a wrinkly, colorful mess. But Sofía has good ideas too. "What do *you* think the new clubhouse should look like?" I ask.

She blinks. "Me?"

"Sure," I say. "You should decide this time, and I'll collect the supplies."

"*¡Michi, michi, michi!*"

Sofía straightens at the sound of a voice coming from up ahead. Her mom is in their front yard, rummaging through the tulips along the house. Her dad is nearby, checking under some bushes.

"*¿Mamá?*" Sofía runs up to her. For a minute, they talk together in Spanish while I catch up with Eli and park the wagon by the front steps. Then Sofía looks over her shoulder at us. "Oriol's gone," she says.

Her dad pats her on the back. "Don't worry, *mija*. He's never missing for long."

It's funny to see Sofía's dad during the day. Usually, he's asleep when I'm here, because he works overnight at a dairy farm. But the family he worked for had to sell their farm a little while ago, and he's been looking for another job.

"We'll go ask the neighbors to keep an eye out for him," her dad says.

Sofía sighs. "Okay."

He and her mom head next door.

"What happened?" Eli asks.

Sofía rolls her eyes. "Oriol ran after a rabbit."

Eli looks worried, but I bet he's thinking about the rabbit, not Oriol. "Don't you keep him in the house?" he asks.

"We used to, but he always wanted to go out, so my dad put a flap on the door. Oriol usually stays in the yard, though." She sighs again.

"He used to be a stray, right?" Eli asks. "Maybe he misses hunting."

She laughs. "Well, he shouldn't. He isn't any good at it. He's always chasing the birds, but he never catches any."

Eli looks relieved at that. "Then he'll probably come back when he's hungry."

Sofía frowns. "I hate it when he runs off."

"I'm sure he's fine," I say.

She bites her lip and looks away.

I glance at Eli.

Here's the thing Sofía doesn't know about Oriol.

I'm not exactly his biggest fan.

I mean, he's handsome and all—sort of sleek and kingly, snowy white with black and orange spots all over. But he isn't even soft. He's actually kind of bristly. He's got this pinchy-looking face too, and all he does is chase the birds and lie around licking himself clean. Every time I pet him, I think about all that licking and feel like I've got cat spit on my hands.

I don't know what Sofía sees in him.

But I know she loves him. A lot. So I don't really have to ask what she wants to do now, because I already know.

"You want us to help you look for him?"

She perks up at that, then lets her shoulders slump. "That's okay. I'm sure he's fine."

I nudge her with my elbow. "Come on, it'll be fun. We'll make it into a game!"

"What kind of game?" asks Eli.

"A contest." I grin. "The first one to find Oriol wins."

3

Oriol might not be my favorite person in the world, but looking for him feels like an adventure.

My wagon creaks and wobbles behind me as we march around the block, checking under bushes and behind trees while Sofía calls for him in Spanish. *"¡Michi, michi, michi! ¡Aquí, gatito!"* I feel important helping her look. I feel like a good friend.

But nobody wins our contest.

By the time Dad calls me home on the walkie-talkie, we still haven't found Oriol. So as soon as I wake up on Sunday morning, I decide to make a wish for him on the Magic Mist.

Rosie is still asleep. Sun is slanting through the blinds, and the color she picked for our room reminds me of the sky after it rains. Our matching Rainbow Ring necklaces are on the nightstand between our beds. I slip mine on and sneak down the hall to my workshop.

There's so much stuff in here that I can barely open the door. Sofía must be right about spring cleaning, because people have been getting rid of the coolest trash ever lately: couch cushions, bicycle tires, stools that are missing rungs, and drawers that are missing dressers. I leave the heavy stuff in the garage, but I lug the rest up here. And now that I have a wagon, I can bring home even more!

We'll be able to make an amazing new clubhouse with all this.

I pick my way across the room and breathe Magic Mist on the window. But suddenly, I realize I have a lot of other wishes inside me too. I don't know which one to pick. Find Oriol? Fix the igloo? Start building the new clubhouse with Sofía? Which one do I want the most? What would a good friend want?

I sigh and trace a kitty in the circle of fog.

I'm on high alert as I creep downstairs. Dad has been pranking me for weeks, and there could be booby traps anywhere. Maybe he built a pyramid of tin cans to come crashing down if I make a wrong move. Or what if he rigged a bucket of water to fall when I open a door? I peek around every corner, watching for trapdoors or springboards.

When I stick my head into the kitchen, Dad is at the stove in his running clothes. Mom is on her computer with papers spread all over the kitchen table. When she sees me, I put my finger to my lips, tiptoe over to the counter, and lift my walkie-talkie from the charger.

My voice blasts through the other handset. "BREAKER, BREAKER, THIS IS BIG ZEE COMING AT YOU!"

Dad jumps and drops the spatula.

I grin and turn down his volume. "Does anybody read me? Over."

Dad picks up his handset and hits the talk button. "Top of the morning to you, Big Zee. Ready to get your eat on? Over."

"That's a big ten-four," I say. "Over."

"Sunny and runny or scrambled? Over."

"Scrambled. Can I have juice, too? Over."

"Affirmative, over."

I grab my pill bottle and settle in at the kitchen table. "Are you working today?" I ask Mom.

She takes off her glasses and does a big stretch. "Almost finished."

I smell the eggs when they start to sizzle in the skillet. When they're ready, Dad sets them in front of me and hands me my sport bottle. I take a sip of juice.

At least I *try* to. Nothing comes out.

I try again. Nothing. I squint at Dad. "What'd you do to my juice?"

He lifts his eyebrows. "Do what now?" he says

into his walkie-talkie. "You're breaking up, over."

I suck on the spout so hard this time that I think my ears will pop. Then I unscrew the lid, look inside, and groan.

There's a mini marshmallow blocking the bottom of the straw.

Mom rolls her eyes as I pluck it off. "April Fools' isn't supposed to last the whole month, you know."

"Tell that to him!" I'm about to open my pill bottle when I stop and look hard at Dad. "There'd better not be one of those spring-snake thingies in here."

Dad lowers his walkie-talkie and smiles. "I wouldn't joke around with your medication."

Maybe not, but I turn the lid slowly anyway. Nothing jumps out, so I tap out a pill and swallow it with a sip of juice.

Wait a second. Maybe *I* should joke around with my medication.

I could pretend to choke on it. That would get him! Better yet, I could pretend it stopped working. I could fall down on the floor and fake a *seizure*.

But I get a funny feeling when I think about squiggling and wriggling on the floor like that. We have two rules about pranks: Nothing Dangerous and Nothing Mean.

I think a fake seizure would be mean.

That's okay. I have a better idea!

I eat my eggs, nice and slow and casual. When I'm finished, I take my dishes to the sink. Then I look out the window and do a big gasp. "Are those Eli's *chickens*?"

But the one who looks up is Mom. "In the yard?" she says. She jumps out of her chair and rushes out the back door.

Dad and I look at each other and start to laugh. When Mom comes back inside, she shakes her head at us. "I don't get you two."

"Sorry," I say. "I know it's not really your thing."

"Pranks?" she says.

"No, fun."

Dad snorts.

Mom stares at me. "I'm plenty fun! I do jigsaw puzzles and crosswords. I listen to podcasts!"

"And wait until you hear her plans for this afternoon," Dad says.

"What plans?"

"Big plans," Dad says. *"Huge."*

Mom pinches her lips together. "If you must know, I'm cleaning the garage."

"Ooo!" I love the garage—the smell of tools and oil, the boxes of Dad's comic books, plastic bins full of who-knows-what. "Can I help?"

She laughs. "You're half the reason it needs to be cleaned in the first place."

"Why?"

"It's so full of your junk, we can't park in there anymore. Your workshop is even worse."

"It's not junk. It's supplies."

"Well, whatever you call it, it's got to go."

"But Sofía and I might need it for our new clubhouse!"

Mom lets out a sigh and comes to tuck my hair behind my ear. "Listen, sweetheart, I don't want to thwart your creativity, but we're up to our eyeballs in trash. We can't live like this."

"I can."

"Well, I can't." She leans over and kisses the top of my head. "I'm going to start on the garage, and I need you to clean up your workshop. Today."

I cross my arms and slump against the sink.

She gets a twinkle in her eyes. "Maybe next weekend, I'll even tackle the storage bins."

Dad laughs. "See? She's plenty fun."

"Who's fun?" Rosie says, shuffling into the kitchen in her nightgown. She's holding Pink Pony with one hand and rubbing her eyes with the other.

"Hey, Rosie," I say, perking up. "Guess what day it is."

She does a little gasp. "Sunday?"

I give her a big grin.

"What are we planting?" she asks, dropping Pink Pony on the table.

I find the bag of mini marshmallows in the

cupboard and wave it in the air. Rosie squeals and races for the door.

"Just watch out for my spinach plants," Mom calls.

We pull on our galoshes and tumble outside. The sun makes each blade of grass glisten as we run through the yard to the garden. It's one of those it's-about-time days in April when the air smells like mulch, and the grass is even greener than it was yesterday. The garden looks like big boxes of mud, but when we get closer, I can see tiny green sprouts coming up in rows.

Rosie's pink plastic hand shovel is still sticking up out of the dirt where she left it last week. "That looks like a good spot," I say, pointing at an empty bed. "You want to dig this time or should I?"

"I'll do it." She plops down on her knees and starts scooping a careful line in the mud.

This is the only prank I'm allowed to play on Rosie, and she doesn't even know it's a prank. I started it a few years ago, after Dad caught me drawing a mustache on her in permanent marker while she slept. That's when he made the Nothing Mean rule for April Fools'.

So I came up with a fun prank instead: the Magic Garden.

Our garden is only magic in April, and only on Sundays. (Mom's rules.) But we've grown all kinds of things—candy canes from peppermints, lollipops from hard candies, and full-size candy bars from chocolate chips. We've grown so many treats that it's getting hard to come up with new ideas!

When Rosie finishes making a little trench, I hand her the bag and watch her drop mini marshmallows into the ground, one at a time. They really do look like giant seeds when you see them in the dirt like that.

"Okay," I say when she's finished. "Cover them up." It hurts a little, watching Rosie pack mud over those perfectly good marshmallows. But it'll be worth it to see her face tomorrow. "Now we just need some of those wooden sticks we use on the grill."

"What for?"

"You know how green beans grow on poles? Marshmallows are like that too. They need something to climb."

We find the skewers in the garage. When we're finished poking them into the ground, Rosie gives the row a gentle pat, like she's petting Eli's rabbit. "Go to sleep, little marshmallows," she whispers. "Grow big and squishy."

"We can check them first thing in the morning," I say.

She stands, her hands and nightgown covered in mud. Then she picks up the bag of mini

marshmallows and gazes at it, looking thoughtful.

"What's up?" I ask.

She tilts her head at me. "Did these grow in a garden too?"

"Where else would they come from?"

"From the store. By the cake-making stuff."

"Well, sure, that's where you *buy* them, but somebody had to pick them first."

"Somebody with a magic garden?"

"Of course. Then they bagged them up and took them to the store. Like potatoes or carrots."

Rosie gives me a doubtful look.

Hang on. She believes me, doesn't she? "What?" I ask.

She blinks a few times. "Nothing."

Then she smiles, hugs me around the stomach, and does her little skip-run back to the house.

After we plant the marshmallows, Mom sends me to clean my workshop.

"But I was going to Eli's to fix the igloo," I tell her.

"You can go when you're done cleaning up," she says.

I let out a huffy breath. "What am I supposed to do? Get rid of *everything*?"

"Of course not. You can keep the things you love."

"I love all of it!"

She sighs. "Then keep the things you're *using*. Get rid of the rest."

I groan and head upstairs, push open the door, and stand with my hands on my hips.

Maybe I can find a *few* things to throw away.

I start kicking things around the floor. I spot a glob of tar that I pulled out of a crack in the street. I guess I'm not using that. But I like it. It's stretchy and speckled with tiny rocks, and it smells like rubber. And what if I don't find any more?

I spot the monster I made out of a shoe box. I guess I'm not using him, either. But he's full of valentines. He looks fierce and colorful and proud of himself. What if getting rid of him hurts his feelings?

I slump into my office chair and spin in a slow circle, looking at my collection. I want to keep it all—the flattened cereal boxes, the keys that don't open anything, the clock I made out of a cracked dinner plate that tells the time every day at four o'clock. Even this chair came home from the curb. Dad carried it up here for me, and it makes me feel like I'm sitting on a throne.

I can't get rid of any of this stuff!

That's when I get an Inspiration.

You know how you can cover your beets with mashed potatoes or move bits of fish around your plate to make it look like you ate your dinner?

That's what I decide to do.

I wad things up, shove them into corners, and push everything against the walls. It takes a while, but I clear enough room to twirl myself around in a circle.

Now I can go to Eli's!

I head downstairs to tell Mom, but when I get to the garage, I see her dragging a rocking chair down the driveway. "Hey, that's mine!" I say.

She stops. "It doesn't have a seat."

"So?"

She sets it down and tightens her ponytail. "So what are you planning to use it for?"

"Sofía might want it for our new clubhouse." I shrug. "She hasn't decided yet."

But Mom picks it back up and takes it to the curb anyway!

And after that, I decide not to go to Eli's at all.

Instead, I spy on Mom as she clatters around in the garage. I lurk nearby when she hauls all my beautiful trash to the curb. I keep watch as she gets rid of my treasures, one by one—the broken stools, the dresser drawers, the flowerpots.

Then I sit in the sandbox plotting, wondering how to get them back.

By the time she's finished for the day, I have a plan.

"Meena?"

I open one eye. Rosie is standing over my bed, her Rainbow Ring dangling from a string around her neck.

"Can we check the garden?" she asks.

I roll onto my other side so she can't see me smile. Then I sit up, stretch, and grab my necklace from the nightstand. "Yeah, okay."

The sun glows orange at the horizon as Rosie does her little fairy run across the yard. The grass is cold against my bare feet and soaks the legs of my pajamas. When we get to the garden, she squeals and jumps for joy. "They grew," she cries, pointing at the jumbo marshmallows on the ends of the skewers.

"Told you," I say with a grin.

She holds out the bottom of her nightgown to make a pouch. While she starts picking, I peek toward the shed. There's a big dirt pile behind it that Mom keeps covered with a giant blue tarp. It's a great hiding place. In all the years I've been playing hide-and-seek with Sofía, she's never found me under there. From here, you can only see the corner of the tarp. You can't tell that it's lumpier than it used to be.

Getting the garden ready wasn't the *only* thing I did after Rosie went to bed last night.

It took a bunch of trips to haul everything around to the backyard with my wagon. I was sweaty and dirty by the time I finished, but my treasures were safe and sound. Technically, I know I'm not using them, but I'm *going* to. Someday. Sofía and I will use them together.

I pop a marshmallow into my mouth.

Rosie's nightgown is full now. "I'm gonna take these for show-and-tell," she says.

"What for? Everybody's seen marshmallows before."

She smiles. "But they don't know about the magic."

I stop chewing. "You can't tell anybody about that."

"Why not?"

I think fast. "It's like making a wish on your birthday. If you tell people, it won't come true."

She nods toward her bundle. "It already came true."

"Yeah, but . . ." I get a weird feeling in my stomach. What would happen if Rosie told the kids in her class about our garden? Would they laugh at her? Would they think she's lying? Would they tell her *I'm* lying?

I love how the garden makes her happy and excited. But if she ends up crying in circle time, then this is a mean prank.

I don't want to do one of those.

"The thing is," I say, "you'll make the other kids jealous. Not everybody has a magic garden, you know."

"But *some* people do."

"Nope," I say. "Just us."

She blinks at me. "Then where did the marshmallows come from?"

"What do you mean? We grew them."

"Not those. The ones we planted." She peers up at me. "You said somebody grew them in a magic garden."

I freeze.

"Didn't they?" she asks.

"Aren't you *glad* we have the only magic garden in the world?" I ask, a little sharper than I mean to.

She shrinks a little and nods.

"Good," I say, relaxing. "Because next Sunday, we're planting something even better than this."

Her face brightens. "What?"

But I don't actually know yet, so I give her a mysterious smile and say, "You'll see."

When we get back to the kitchen, Dad looks up from his coffee. "What have you got there?" he asks.

Rosie holds out her nightgown to show him.

"Whoa, that's quite a crop!"

She stuffs two marshmallows into her mouth at once.

"Hey, now," Mom says, opening the blinds. "That's too much sugar first thing in the morning."

Rosie shrugs. "They grew in the garden. So they must be vegetables."

Dad laughs. "Hard to argue with that."

"Oh my goodness," Mom says suddenly, peering out the window.

"What?" I ask.

"All our trash is gone." She chuckles and shakes her head. "You never know what some people will pick up off the curb."

Mom hasn't tried to get rid of my wagon yet, but I'm not taking any chances. So when Rosie and I leave for school, I bring it along.

Eli rides up as I'm parking it by the bike rack. "Is the igloo okay?" I ask, gripping the handle tighter.

"So far," he says. "It's still crooked, but I put big cans of tomatoes around the umbrella handle. I think that'll hold it for a while."

I let out a breath. "Okay, thanks."

We get through our morning routine and language arts. I race with Pedro at first recess while Sofía plays ponies with Nora. After math, we head to lunch. I'm about to ask Sofía to trade when I notice something.

She packed a very un-Sofía lunch today. It's nothing but a couple of flappy-cheese sandwiches and a banana. I don't even see an apple juice can, even though she always gives me the tab. "Where's your juice?" I ask.

"We ran out."

"Why didn't you buy more?"

She sighs. "We have to wait until my dad gets a new job."

"Oh." I look down at my lunch bag. Is apple juice expensive? What else is different in Sofía's house since her dad isn't working? "Can't he just go work on another farm?" I ask.

She frowns. "He liked working for a family. Dad says the only farms left are like big companies. They have thousands of cows. He wouldn't even get a chance to know them. Plus he'd get paid less, but he'd have to work even more."

Huh. That doesn't sound fair. I break my cookie in half and hand her a piece. "Did you at least find Oriol?"

She shakes her head. "We kept calling for him all weekend, but . . ." She gives me a worried look. "Do you think something happened to him?"

"Nah. My mom always thinks something happened to *me* when she calls and I don't come. But it's not like I fell off a cliff or anything. I just don't want to stop what I'm doing." I hand her the rest of my cookie. "I bet Oriol just felt like a vacation. I bet he's dozing on the beach right now, or maybe going for a swim!"

That makes her giggle. "I doubt it. He hates the water."

"Then he's off chasing birds he'll never catch. He'll be back. You just need something to take your mind off it."

"Like what?"

I waggle my eyebrows at her. "Like a project."

Sofía laughs. The sound reminds me of bubbles, floating gently into the air. I like making her feel better.

"How about we start planning the new clubhouse?" I say. "I've got *tons* of supplies."

Sofía makes a face. "You mean like the stuff you found the other day?"

I blink. "Yeah, why?"

She works her jaw back and forth. "It's kind of big, isn't it?"

Doesn't she *want* that?

I chew on the inside of my cheek. What if she doesn't? I'm supposed to be a good friend and listen to her ideas this time. I'm supposed to do what *she* wants.

I rub the back of my neck. "I mean, I have smaller stuff too. Bottle caps, twist ties, Popsicle sticks . . ."

"What else?"

I hesitate. I have plenty of trash to choose from, but Sofía is looking at me like it isn't enough.

What else is there?

I look around the lunchroom. All around me, kids are stuffing wrappers into lunch bags and dumping their trays on their way to recess. My

eyes zoom in on all those milk cartons and pudding cups going into the trash—all those chip bags
and yogurt sleeves and cupcake holders.

A slow smile spreads across my face.

I know supplies when I see them.

And I have a wagon now.

5

My wagon screeches behind me as I wheel my new treasures home. Mom is out back when I get there, so I sneak everything up to my workshop without her seeing.

On Tuesday, I bring my wagon to school again. I circle the tables at lunch, collecting mini straws, plastic sporks, tinfoil lids—anything I think Sofía might want to use for our project. Then, on my way to recess, I slow down to look at the Lost and Found table. A lot of this stuff has been sitting here forever: metal rings from a broken binder, a pencil box with a busted hinge, sparkly pens that are out of ink. If anybody wanted it, they would have taken it by now. I check to make sure nobody's looking before I scoop it all up.

When school is over, I skip out the door swinging a plastic bag in each hand. "I don't know why I never built anything out of milk cartons before," I tell Sofía as I load the bags into my wagon. "They're like baby milk jugs! I bet they'd make a great club-house."

She loads the bags she's carrying for me but doesn't answer.

We head down the sidewalk, the wagon squealing behind us. "I bet if we turn them on their sides, they'll stack like bricks. We could even paint them different colors!"

Sofía stays quiet, but she has on her doing-fractions frown.

She's been weird all day, actually. She didn't sing in music class. She got out first when we played elimination in gym because she wasn't watching the ball. She didn't even want any of my Flaming Crunchers at lunch, even though they were the Red Firebird flavor! "What's the matter?" I ask.

She glances at me then down at the sidewalk. "It's Oriol."

Oh, is that all. "Still at the beach?" I ask.

She twists her long braid into a rope. "I stayed outside calling him until bedtime last night."

I stop. "You're not really worried, are you?"

"I *wasn't*," she says. "But it's been three days! He's never gone this long."

"Want me to help you look some more? Check the parks or something?"

"Mom and I have been doing that every day."

I see the way her face is pinching up, and I want

to make her feel better like before. "Then why don't I come over? I could at least keep you company while you wait for him to show up."

She lets out a breath. "Okay."

I shrug off my backpack and dig out my walkie-talkie. "Big Zee to Mama Zee," I say. "Come in, Mama Zee, over."

After a minute, Mom's voice crackles through the speaker. "Hi, honey."

"Big Zee," I remind her. "You're supposed to use my call handle, over."

There's a pause. "Do you need something?" she asks.

"I'm headed to the Flamingo's, over."

"Any homework?"

"You didn't say over, over."

"Over," she says.

I slap my forehead. "You say it when you're done talking, over."

There's a long pause. "Do you have any homework or don't you?"

"Negatory, over."

"Then I'll call you when it's time for dinner. Have fun."

"Ten-four, Mama Zee. Over and out."

Sofía's mom greets us at the door. Her smile seems a little faded today, like a light turned down to dim.

Sofía's dad is on a computer at the kitchen table. *"Mi corazón,"* he says, opening his arms.

Sofía moves into his hug. "Did you find anything?"

"Not yet." He squeezes her tight. "But there are more jobs out there."

She looks toward the back door, standing open. "What about Oriol?"

Her dad gives her *I'm sorry* eyes. "I'm sure it won't be long now. You'll see."

I follow Sofía into the yard. She makes a clicking sound with her teeth. *"Michi, michi, michi,"* she calls. *"¡Aquí, gatito!"* We check the bushes and flower beds, but I don't think either of us expects to find him.

"You want to start our new clubhouse?" I ask when we head back inside. "I've got milk cartons and pudding cups and all kinds of little straws and things."

She shrugs. "If you want."

I stare at her. "Don't *you* want?"

She shifts from one foot to the other. "Can we make something else? Something that won't take as long?"

"Like what?"

"I don't know. Maybe bird feeders? I have a couple of jugs."

"Don't you want to use the stuff I collected?"

"We can if you want."

I have to stop myself from groaning out loud.

This is *not* what I have in mind. Anybody can make a bird feeder. I want to make something *big*, something amazing. And I want to use the trash I brought!

But if this is what she wants ... I feel my shoulders slumping. I guess a good friend would be fine with that.

Maybe it can be our warm-up project.

I stuff my hands in the front pocket of my hoodie and cross my fingers as tight as I can. "Bird feeders would be nice," I say.

Sofía gets the jugs, and we settle in at the table across from her dad. We tie strings to the handles and cut holes in the sides so the birds can hop in. She uses blue and black markers to cover her jug with little rectangles that look like stained glass— blue jay feathers, I realize. I get rolls of duct tape from her craft drawer and cover my jug in rainbow stripes. They're crooked, but I don't care.

We aren't even working together. We're working next to each other. Every few minutes, Sofía goes to look outside. Every time she comes back, she seems farther away. Finally, she finishes her jug, fills it with dry oatmeal, and hangs it in the yard. Then she rests her head in her arms and watches me wrap purple tape around my feeder. The only sound is the click of computer keys and the squeak of the tape coming off the roll. Once, Sofía's mom asks her dad something. He answers in a tight voice then flashes a smile and squeezes her hand.

Suddenly, a phone vibrates. Sofía's dad jumps up and grabs it from the table. *"Hermano, ¿qué tal?"* he says, hurrying down the hall. I hear a door close, and his voice becomes muffled.

Sofía's mom paces for a minute then stops at the little altar in the corner. There are two dried palm crosses hanging on the wall behind it. Sofía and I made those a few weeks ago. She got the palm leaves at her church when they were still green, and her mom showed us how to fold them. I was pretty proud of my cross . . . until I saw her mom weave a little basket. Her hands moved so fast that I couldn't keep track of what they were doing! It's on the altar now, next to a glowing glass candle. I watch Sofía's mom clutch her hands in front of it and squeeze her eyes shut, like she's making a wish.

Just then, Sofía's dad bursts back into the room. "Sofía *mía*," he cries, grinning. "How would you like to see your cousins?"

She gasps. "Really?"

He nods, his eyes sparkling.

She launches herself into his arms. Her mom laughs as he whirls Sofía around, and all at once, it's like the place is full of music, even though nobody is singing a note.

Then Sofía is on her feet again, breathless and beaming. "They're really coming *here*?"

Her dad's smile catches. "No, *mija*. We're going there."

Again? My heart sinks. Sofía lived in California when she was little, and her family still goes to visit. But they just went over winter break.

Sofía is jumping up and down now. "When? When?"

"Soon. A couple of weeks."

She stops. "I'll miss school?"

Lucky!

"You'll make it up," her dad says.

Her mother starts talking then, her voice fast and happy and melodic.

Sofía's eyes go wide. She takes a step backward.

I'm about to snip the purple tape, but I lower my scissors. Her mom rubs Sofía's arms up and down, saying something soothing.

"It's not for sure yet," her dad says. "But it's good news, yes?" He turns to Sofía's mom. *"Vamos a llamar a mi madre, ¿sí?"* They each kiss Sofía on the cheek before they disappear down the hall again.

Sofía stares after them.

"What was that all about?" I ask.

She turns to me, looking dazed. "He found a job."

"Oh, good! Now you can buy apple juice. What's he gonna do?"

She blinks fast. "He's going to help run his brother's store."

For some reason, I feel a tingle on the bottoms of my feet when she says that. "I thought you didn't have any family around here."

"We don't," she says. "They're in California."

"Then why does he have a store here?"

She bites her lip.

Wait a second.

I drop my scissors. A cold feeling whooshes over me, like someone rigged a bucket of ice water to fall on my head. "You mean they'd make you *move*?"

"I don't know," she says, her voice rising. "Mom said he's still looking at jobs here, but—"

Relief floods through my body, all the way down to my toes. "So it's just a backup plan. There are tons of things he could do. He could be a trapeze artist! We don't have a single one of those in this town. Or any train conductors. Or he could wear an ape suit and hold a sign when stores are having a sale!"

Sofía smiles weakly.

"Maybe he'll even find a job during the day this time. Then he'll be home at night."

Suddenly, a chirping sound comes through the back door: *"Ack-ack-ack!"*

We look at each other. *Oriol?*

We scrape back our chairs and scramble outside in time to see a brown squirrel streak across the yard. Sofía stops short as it skitters up a tree. Then she makes a whimpering sound and sinks to the stoop.

I sit next to her. I don't know what to say, so I just press my shoulder against hers. She leans against me, the worry coming off of her like heat. I can tell she's thinking about Oriol, but is she thinking about California, too?

A little red-and-brown bird flits across the yard and lands in Sofía's feeder. I point, hoping to take her mind off of everything. "Look." She glances up. The checkered jug spins from a clothesline pole as the bird pecks at the oats inside. "What kind of bird is that?" I ask.

"A house finch," Sofía says in a dull voice.

There's a flutter in a nearby bush—a bunch of birds making squeaky, tweeting sounds. "And what are those?"

She sighs. "Sparrows."

I blink at her. "You didn't even look."

"But that's what they sound like when they're together. Sparrows are always part of a flock."

A black-and-white bird swoops for the feeder. "What's that?" I ask.

"A black-capped chickadee." Sofía looks around. "There's probably another one."

Sure enough, I spot a second one on the branch nearby. "How did you know that?"

"Because they're partner birds," she says. "You almost never see one without the other."

For a minute, we don't say anything while the birds twitter and flit. Then I loop my pinky through her friendship bracelet. "Are you okay?"

She takes a shuddery breath but doesn't answer.

My stomach starts to squeeze tight. Now *I'm* thinking about California.

I give myself a little shake. *No.* Sofía can't move. We have playdates on Fridays and meetings on Saturdays. We have treasures to find and projects to make and a new clubhouse to build!

But she can't think about any of those things while she's worrying about her cat.

And I'm her best friend. If anybody should help find him, it's me.

I sit up straighter. "Do you think our parents would post Oriol's picture online?"

She looks at me. "I think so."

"What if we made posters too? Something to hang around town."

She nods slowly. "We could take them to the vet. And the animal shelter."

"We could stick them in mailboxes," I say. "We could even take them to school."

She blinks a few times. "You think people will help us look for him?"

"Of course they will. It'll be like our own

personal spy network. The bigger the better."

She gets to her feet, her face bright. "My dad has pictures on his phone."

I stand up. "Then let's go find Oriol."

We head inside. Sofía hurries down the hall. I hear her talking to her parents in Spanish. Across the room, the candle flickers. I go to stand in front of it. On the glass, there's a picture of a brown lady surrounded by sunbeams. A flame dances inside, about where her heart would be.

Sofía can't leave me. She *can't*.

I close my eyes and make a wish.

6

We design the poster together.

Sofía blows up a picture of Oriol on the computer, and I type LOST CAT in big letters at the top. She adds GATO PERDIDO at the bottom with a phone number, and we print out a stack. The ink is black, so I outline the letters in rainbow while Sofía colors Oriol's orange spots.

It's not as good as making a new clubhouse, but I guess that can wait until we find him.

When Mom calls me home, I bring some posters with me and slip them into mailboxes along the way. I keep an eye out for Oriol, too. But after a while, thoughts start to squeal inside my head as loudly as the wagon behind me.

Thoughts about California.

I don't want to think about that. So I try to find every color of the rainbow instead. Between the tulips and the violets and the daffodils, I've got all my colors in no time. I breathe them in and let them fill me up until I'm home. Then I pull my wagon around back to stash my lunchroom treasures under the tarp.

"Meena!" Rosie waves to me from the sandbox. "Come see my castle!"

"Just a sec." I grab the striped jug out of my wagon and find a tree near the garden to hang it.

Rosie wanders over in her yellow galoshes and a pair of fairy wings. "What's that?"

"A bird feeder."

She gives it a little spin. "It's pretty."

I smile. The stripes are still crooked, and I didn't have enough orange tape to go all the way around, but Rosie likes everything I make.

I glance around for Oriol as she leads me to the sandbox. It's not actually a box. It's an old tractor tire with sand in the middle. Rosie made a pretty good castle. It's even got a tower with a dried leaf for a flag on top and Pink Pony standing guard.

"Nice," I say, peeking back at my wagon. I can't get to the tarp with Rosie hanging around, but Mom will see me if I try to get the bags up to my workshop.

"And look what Eli gave me," Rosie says. She reaches into her pocket and holds up a baggie of seeds and pellets.

"What's that?"

"Chicken feed. To plant in our magic garden."

My eyebrows shoot straight up. "What are you planning to grow?"

She tilts her head at me, like I should know. "Baby chicks."

I laugh. "That's not where chicks come from. They hatch from eggs."

Rosie scoffs. "There are no chickens inside *our* eggs."

"That's because . . . ," I stop. Huh. Why *don't* our eggs have chickens in them?

She waves the baggie in front of my face. "Can we plant it?" she asks. *"Pleeease?"*

I finger the Rainbow Ring on my necklace, thinking. There's no way we can plant that stuff. Pretending to grow marshmallows is one thing. But *chickens*? "I mean, we could," I say slowly, "but Mom would never let us keep the chicks." I lean in closer. "She might even make us *eat* them."

Rosie gasps. "She would not."

I shrug. "Where do you think chicken nuggets come from?"

She slaps a hand over her mouth.

Just then, my walkie-talkie crackles to life. "Zee Money to Big Zee. Got your ears on? Over."

I unclip it from my waistband and press the talk button. "Big Zee here. Go ahead, over."

"Come on in for some grub. And bring your tag-along, over."

"Copy that, Zee Money. Over and out." I hook the walkie-talkie on my pants again and turn to

Rosie. "Listen, if you really don't mind eating the chickens—"

She shakes her head. "I'm not eating baby chicks!"

I wrap an arm around her and head toward the house. "Then let's think of something else to plant."

"Tacos?" she says.

"Too messy."

"Ice cream cones?"

"They'd melt before we picked them."

"Donuts?"

I stop.

Rosie bounces on her toes. "Can we? I love donuts!"

I grin. "Then donuts it is."

Stir fry is usually one of my favorite dinners, because Dad mixes in a whole rainbow of vegetables. But right when I'm about to take a bite, the wheel in my mind starts squeaking about California again.

No, I tell myself. Sofía's dad will find a job here. There are plenty of other farms he could work on. Or he could tame lions! He could judge cupcakes on TV! He could dress scarecrows or dig up dinosaurs or clean out wishing pennies from fountains. Heck, once I get thinking about it, I can't *stop* coming up with job ideas.

I relax and dig into some pea pods. "Did Sofía's

dad send you a message?" I ask when Mom passes me the hot sauce.

"About her cat?"

"Yeah. Can you share it online?"

"Sure."

"And I have posters for you to take to work," I say to Dad.

"Copy that," he says.

Rosie's fork clinks as she pokes at her bowl. "Are there any chickens in this?" she asks.

Uh-oh.

Mom and Dad look at each other.

She sets down her fork. "I'm not eating any chickens."

"It's okay, squirt," I say quickly. "I'm sure it's nobody we know."

She crosses her arms and shakes her head.

Mom sighs. "Eat the vegetables, then."

I take a big forkful to show Rosie how good they are. "Yum." I nudge her with my elbow, scoop up another bite, and—

Wait a second.

Is that a marshmallow in my stir fry?

Dad.

I look right at him, stab it with my fork, and swallow it whole.

He looks back at me, picks up a mini corn on the cob, and nibbles it straight across.

For the rest of dinner, my mind is busy with a zillion things. One blob of brain is trying to think of a new prank for Dad. Another hunk is thinking of places to hang our posters. A spot in the back is still coming up with job ideas. And one whole chunk is wondering how to get those lunch treasures up to my workshop.

But when we start clearing the dishes, I see Mom tie up the kitchen trash, and suddenly my brain solves two problems at once.

Sometimes I could just kiss that thing!

I slip Dad's walkie-talkie off the charger, clip it next to mine, and pull my hoodie down over them both. As soon as I see Mom lift the bag out of the wastebasket, I hurry over. "Oh, is it trash night?" I ask, nice and casual. "I'll take it out for you."

She raises her eyebrows at me. "Why?"

I bat my eyelashes. "Just to be helpful."

"You won't try to keep any of it?"

"Pshhh." I wave my hand in the air. "What would I want with a bunch of banana peels and coffee grounds?"

"Beats me." She hands me the bag and points at me. "No funny business."

I trace an X over my chest and cross my fingers with the other hand.

"Hey, Rosie," I say. "Will you get the door for me?"

She stops pushing in chairs and glances up.

I give her a big wink.

Her whole face lights up. She peeks at Mom and Dad then scurries ahead of me.

"Leave the door open," I whisper as we step outside. I heave the bag into the big trash bin and roll it to the curb. Then I unclip Dad's walkie-talkie, turn the volume all the way up, and set it inside the bin, right on top of the bag.

"Ready?" I ask.

Rosie grins. "Ready."

I cup my hands around my mouth. "Mom, Dad," I shout. "Come quick!"

I grab Rosie's hand and take off. We run around the house and head straight for my wagon. "Get those bags," I say. "Hurry!"

She takes one in each hand. I grab the others and peek through the back door. The kitchen is empty now, the front door standing open.

"Meena?" I hear Mom calling from out front.

"Upstairs," I tell Rosie. "Come on!"

We clobber up the stairs, toss the bags into my workshop, and slam the door. Then I grab my own walkie-talkie. "Over here," I whine into the mic.

I race to our bedroom and stop at the front window. Mom and Dad are on the sidewalk below, looking confused.

I press the talk button again. "In here! We fell in!"

Mom and Dad look right at the bin.

I giggle and hold the walkie-talkie up to Rosie. "Help, help," she cries.

Mom and Dad grab for the lid. They open it, look inside, and—

Dad bursts out laughing.

We clap our hands and shriek with laughter as Mom picks up his walkie-talkie. Then I knock on the window until they look up. Rosie and I stick out our tongues and wiggle our fingers in our ears.

Mom rolls her eyes. Dad grins and shakes his fist.

I got him! I got them both!

And I got all my trash upstairs to my workshop, safe and sound and out of sight.

On Wednesday morning, I keep an eye out for Oriol as we walk to school. Rosie helps me check the recycling bins on the way. I load up my wagon with milk jugs, egg cartons, aluminum cans—anything I think Sofía and I might use for our new clubhouse someday.

As soon as I get to the playground, she runs up to me, waving a stack of fliers. "I have enough for our whole class," she says. "And the secretary said if Oriol isn't back by Friday, we can send them home with the whole *school*."

When the bell rings, we hurry inside and find Mrs. D. "Can we do show-and-tell today?" I ask as kids file into our room.

She raises her eyebrows. "I bet you haven't done that since kindergarten. Do you have something to share?"

I hand her one of our fliers. "Please?"

Mrs. D looks it over and gives Sofía a kind

smile. "I'll save you a few minutes at the end of the day."

I hate waiting. But at least we get to use clay in art class and run relay races in gym. Plus I collect even more treasures at lunch. Finally, we get to our last subject, social studies.

Mrs. D has us grab laptops and pair up. "Next year," she says, "you'll be learning about our home state, but today, I'd like you and your partner to research another state. You can pick one you've visited, one you'd like to visit, or just someplace you want to know more about."

"I get Chicago," Lin calls.

"Chicago is a city," Mrs. D says. "But it's in the state of Illinois. You may pick that if you like."

"What about New York?" Aiden asks. "Is that a city or a state?"

"It's both, actually."

Other kids start piping up. "What about Alaska? Georgia? Miami?"

Mrs. D holds up her hands. "If you're not sure, you can look it up. Or feel free to consult our handy-dandy, in-class resource."

Everyone looks at one another.

She gestures toward the reading corner, at the United States rug that's stretched across the floor. "You've been arguing all year about who gets to sit in Oregon and who's stuck way out in Maine."

Huh. It turns out I already know a bunch of states just from picking my spot on the rug. I usually like to sprawl out in the roomy ones like Texas or Montana. Or sometimes I like to plop down in Vermont and see how many states I can sit on at once. And if I want to sit where Mrs. D can't see me? Well, then I head straight for the Carolinas.

Hang on. I learned all those states without my permission!

Mrs. D is sneakier than I thought.

When she starts passing out the worksheets, I turn to Sofía. "Let's do Rhode Island. It's tiny, so we shouldn't have to write very much."

"Actually, can we do California?"

I have to stop myself from groaning out loud. The thought of that place makes my brain squeal with worry. Besides, it's one of the biggest states on the rug! But I'm letting her have more picks, so I take a big breath and let it out. "Yeah, okay."

Sofía puts our names on the worksheet and draws the shape of California in the square. I start looking up answers to the fill-in-the-blank questions. "Let's see. Abbreviation . . ."

"C-A," Sofía says.

I look and see she already wrote it. "Oh. Okay, capital city . . ." I click on the keyboard. "Sacramento."

She jots it down.

"State bird . . ." I pull up a picture of a speckled gray bird with a round body. "The California valley quail."

Sofía looks at the screen. "Oh, I love those!"

"What's that on its head?" I ask. It's like the red thing that hangs off a turkey, only it's black and sticking straight up.

"That's its plume," Sofía says. She reaches over and clicks on a video. A flock of quails starts bobbing along, pecking at the ground. Then all at once, they start running. They look exactly like gray cartoon pears on a whirl of legs.

Sofía grins. "Quails are so funny. They're nervous all the time. And if something startles one of them, the whole flock takes off." She giggles. "Elena likes to jump out at them."

"Who's Elena?"

"One of my cousins."

"One of them?" I look at her. "Do you have a lot?"

She starts counting on her fingers. "Eight cousins, three aunts, two uncles, and two bulldogs." She brightens. "Elena is my age, and everyone says we look like twins. Mom says if we move there, we'll even be in the same class."

My stomach tightens. "Your dad's still looking at jobs here, though, right?"

"Yeah."

"Because I have a lot of ideas if he needs them."

She turns back to the worksheet. I look over her shoulder and see a fill-in-the-blank for time. I check the clock, pull the paper in front of me, and write *2:40*.

"That's not right." She pulls it back. "It's only *twelve* forty there."

"You're telling me California is in the *past*?" I reach for the worksheet again.

She covers it with her arms. "It's in a different time zone. After the sun comes up here, it takes two more hours before it rises there."

Geez. California sounds like another *planet*. I press my lips together as she writes *Pacific Time* then turn back to the computer. "We need some Fun Facts."

For the next few minutes, I click away while Sofía starts filling out the Fun Facts section at the bottom of the page. She hums while she works. I feel my eyebrows wrinkling.

"Find anything?" she asks finally.

Did I ever!

I lean back in my seat. "First of all," I say, "there are *way* more people in California than there are here, and almost all of them are strangers, which everyone knows you're not supposed to talk to."

Sofía blinks. "It's not really—"

"Plus California is *huge*," I say. "It's one of the biggest states in the country, so it's probably really easy to get lost. And do you think any of those strangers would come looking for you?" I shake my head.

"And another thing," I say. "Did you know that California hardly gets any snow? That means no snowball fights, no sledding, and *no snow days*! They also have *earthquakes* there. California has, like, ten thousand earthquakes a *year*!"

"But you can't even feel most of them," Sofía says.

I cross my arms. "You're telling me you can't feel it when the ground cracks open and swallows buildings *whole*?"

"It's not like that," Sofía says. "Most of the time, you don't even know when an earthquake is happening. Or you feel a vibration, but it's so small you think you imagined it."

I stare at her. "You've been to an earthquake?"

"Lots of them."

"You never told me that!"

She shrugs. "It's no big deal."

I snap the computer shut. "Can you just write down my Fun Facts so we can be done?"

"I didn't tell you mine yet."

"You didn't look anything up."

"I didn't have to. I lived there until I was five. And we go to visit every year!"

I push away the computer. "Fine. What are they?"

She picks up the paper. "First of all, Disney is there."

"Not the good Disney."

She looks hard at me. "You've never been to any of the Disneys."

I scowl.

"Also, the tallest trees in the world grow there."

"And I sure wouldn't want *those* things falling on me," I mutter.

Sofía rolls her eyes and turns back to our paper. "California is right next to the ocean, too," she says. "There are tons of beaches and waterbirds, and the weather is so nice that I can rollerblade with my cousins all year. It's not just my mom and dad and me when we're there, either. We're a whole *flock* of family. We eat and play and go to church together, and we hang out at everyone's houses, and it doesn't even matter that I don't live there, because when I'm with them, it feels like home."

Sofía's cheeks are pink by the time she finishes. Her eyes are bright too. They're so bright I have to look away.

She has a whole other life there, I realize suddenly. And she *likes* it.

Better than she likes her life here?

The thought makes my stomach feel like it's full of quicksand.

I look over at the story-time rug. Sofía likes to sit on California when Mrs. D reads to us. But even when we're on opposite sides of the map, she's never more than a few steps away.

What if she really lived there? How far away would she be then?

She's starting to feel far away already.

"Time's up, everyone," Mrs. D says.

Sofía hands me the worksheet, but I don't bother adding my Fun Facts. Everyone scrapes their desks back into place as Mrs. D picks up our papers. "Are you two ready to make your announcement?" she asks.

Geez, I forgot all about Oriol. That doesn't seem like something a good friend would do.

I take a breath and give myself a shake. So what if Sofía likes California? She can like it all she wants when she visits.

But she lives *here* now, where I am. I'm still her best friend, and I'm going to act like it.

Mrs. D quiets the class. We step to the front of the room. For a few seconds, Sofía gets shy, so I hold up one of our fliers to get us started. "Sofía's cat is missing," I say then nudge her with my elbow.

She clears her throat. "He's white with patches all over. They're the same colors as an oriole bird, so I gave him the same name."

I lower the flier. "Really? That's why?"

She looks surprised. "Yeah. And I wanted his name to sound the same in English and Spanish, like mine does."

Huh. I didn't know that. I guess I never asked.

She turns back to the class. "We've been looking for him all week, but we need help."

I start passing out the fliers. "Hang these up anywhere you can. Show them to your family too."

Kids look closely at the picture of Oriol, like they're trying to memorize his face.

"If you think you see him," Sofía says, "call that number."

I wave the extra fliers in the air. "Anybody want another one?"

Every kid in the class raises a hand.

Sofía and I grin at each other. I cross my fingers and hope this works!

8

I'm almost positive we'll find Oriol now that our whole class is looking for him. But when I ask around on Thursday, no one has spotted him yet. There's no sign of him Friday, either. Our poster goes home with all the other classes, like the secretary promised. After school, Sofía and I spend our whole playdate tromping through neighborhoods, leaving fliers in mailboxes, and calling for Oriol everywhere we go.

At least she doesn't mention California again.

Finally, it's Saturday: club day. Something *I* want to do for a change.

It's warm and windy on the way to Eli's. The sky is full of those cotton-ball clouds you see before a storm. I leave a flier at every house I pass and then check on the igloo.

It's even more crooked now. It slants so far to the left that the right side is lifting off the floor! But at least the roof is holding up. For a minute, I stand on the back porch and watch the pine trees swaying in the wind. I hope our igloo is like the trees. I hope it bends but doesn't break.

When Aunt Kathy lets me in, I find Eli in his room, spreading hay for his guinea pig. He has every kind of pet you can imagine in here—tanks of reptiles, cages of rodents. It's like a miniature zoo.

I crinkle my nose. It kind of smells like one too.

I check the whiteboard he uses to keep track of his pet chores. "Want me to feed the fish?" I ask.

"Sure," he says.

I sprinkle pellets over Lizzy's aquarium. She doesn't look that great. Lizzy used to be bright blue. Her fins would ripple like there was a breeze blowing through the water, and she'd zip to the top of the tank for her food. But now she's just sitting there, looking faded. I tap the glass.

"Don't do that," Eli says, coming to stand next to me. "It stresses her out."

I watch her gills flutter. "I guess she's getting close to her expiration date."

He sighs. "I can't tell if she's sick or just old. I'm gonna clean her tank tomorrow and see if that helps."

I don't know what to say. I mean, when you have as many pets as Eli, somebody's always kicking the bucket. I guess he must be used to it by now.

We're filling the last of the water bowls when Sofía arrives.

"Any luck?" Eli asks.

She shakes her head sadly. "A few people sent pictures of stray cats, but they didn't look anything like Oriol." She frowns. "It's been a whole week now. Where could he be?"

Eli sets down the water pitcher. "I have some ideas."

"You do?"

"Yeah." He grabs *All About Cats* from his bookshelf. He's got the whole *All About Animals* set with volumes on snakes, mice, hermit crabs . . . pretty much everything. "I've been trying to figure out where Oriol might have gone," Eli says.

"What'd you find out?" I ask.

He starts paging through the book. "Well, most cats stay close to home. They don't go more than a couple of blocks away. But some have a really big territory. They might go a mile or two, especially if they used to be a stray."

"Two *miles*?" Sofía asks.

"But if they leave their territory, they can get lost."

"Why would they leave?" I ask.

"They might chase something too far. Or something might chase them."

"Then what?" Sofía asks.

"Most cats hide for a while then try to get back."

Sofía bites her lip. "What if Oriol can't find his way?"

"He probably will, but it could take a while." Eli lights up. "I read about this one family that lost their cat while they were on vacation. They couldn't find her anywhere, so they had to go home without her. But a couple of months later, she showed up on their doorstep. She walked, like, two hundred miles, but somehow she found her way back!"

Sofía looks upset. "Do you think Oriol could have gone that far?"

"No way," I say. "Even if he went a couple of miles, he'd still be in town."

"Then what's taking him so long?" Sofía asks.

Eli shrugs. "He might still be hiding. Or maybe someone else started feeding him. Then he wouldn't be in a hurry to come back."

"But *we* feed him," Sofía says.

"Yeah, but some cats have more than one home. Look at this!" He turns to a picture of a gray tabby. "This cat had five different families! He went from house to house every day, and nobody knew it. They all thought he was their cat!"

"So whose was he?" I ask.

Eli grins. "He was *his*."

Sofía's eyes go wide. "You think Oriol has another family?"

"So what if he does," I say. "You have another

family in California. But when you visit, you always come back, because this is your *real* home."

She bites her lip.

I grab pinkies with her. "Oriol would never leave his best friend."

Sofía pinches up her face, like she's trying not to cry.

Eli and I look at each other. "Here," he says, opening a cage. "Hold Vernon. It'll make you feel better." He lifts out his rabbit and places him in Sofía's arms. She takes a shaky breath, nuzzles him against her cheek, and starts rocking him.

Eli reaches into a bin and holds out a few lettuce leaves. Vernon begins nibbling them.

Sofía strokes his long ears. "Did you find out anything else?"

"Did you know that cats clean themselves for two or three hours a day?"

She smiles. "I could have told you that."

"And their brains are only as big as an egg."

"Really?"

"And some people think their noses are all different from each other, like fingerprints. And when they—"

"Can we start our club now?" I ask.

All this cat talk is making me itchy.

But Sofía just looks at me. "I didn't look for birds this week," she says.

"What? Why not?"

She stiffens. "Because I was looking for Oriol."

I turn to Eli. "What about you?"

"I didn't collect anything either, but I'm *about* to." He starts bouncing in place. He has that sparkle in his eye that he gets whenever—

Oh, no.

Sofía gasps. "What are you getting?"

"Guess."

"A lizard? A ferret?"

"Nope." He looks at me.

Ugh. "I don't know. A bird?"

He frowns. "I'd never keep a bird in a cage."

"What do you mean? You have chickens."

"That's different. Chickens can't fly."

I roll my eyes. "Just tell us what you're getting."

He throws out his arms. "A rabbit!"

"Another one?"

"Vernon needs a friend," he says, scratching him behind the ears.

"I thought Aunt Kathy said you couldn't get another pet until something died."

Eli's face falls a little. "Henry did."

"Which one was that?"

Sofía elbows me. "His hamster."

"Oh." I shift on my feet. "Sorry." But I mean, I'm not *that* sorry, because I'm pretty sure Henry peed on me once.

"I got a new rabbit hutch, too. We just have to put it together. Wanna see?" He drops down to his knees and drags a big, flat box out from under his bed. The picture on the front shows a hutch with two levels and a little play area.

Sofía strokes the top of Vernon's head. "Look at that," she says. "It'll be like your own little apartment!"

I glance around. The room is already crowded with tanks and cages. "Where are you gonna put that thing?"

"On the back porch."

"The chicken coop is there."

He gives me a guilty look.

I suck in a breath. "No."

"Meena—"

"We just built it!"

"We didn't *just*. It's been up for months."

"But it's our club headquarters!"

"And it's falling apart."

Sofía looks back and forth between us. "Could we move it?"

Eli looks doubtful. "Maybe."

I cross my arms. "It's fine where it is."

"It's fine for *now*. We have to get rid of it sometime."

I stomp my foot. "We're not getting rid of it!" I storm from the room, down the hall, and out the back door. Then I stand with my hands on my hips, gazing at our lopsided igloo.

There must be some way to keep it safe.

I guess if I took it to my house, we could have our meetings there until we build the new club-house at Sofía's. But can I move it? I sit and give the base a gentle push with my feet. The bottom jugs start to slide, but the ones on top sway in the other direction. I pull back before the dome collapses.

Maybe I could try sliding a big sheet of card-board underneath and dragging it. But how would I ever get it down the porch steps?

I can't give up on it now! It might not be per-fect, but it's *ours*. It's the best thing I ever made.

I won't let anything happen to it.

I run into the kitchen and grab a roll of duct tape from the junk drawer. Then I make a big yel-low X between the pillars, marking off this whole side of the porch. I get a black magic marker and write across the tape: *Danger! Keep out!*

The igloo looks off-limits now, but I crawl through the door anyway. It's crowded in here with the bucket holding up the umbrella that's holding up the roof. I lie down and curl onto my side.

The wind is blowing even harder than before. The chickens make nervous clucking sounds in the coop. A big gust bursts through the pines, and somewhere inside the house, a door slams.

I reach into the pocket of my hoodie and feel for the things I brought with me today: a broken checker, half of a watchband, and the handle of a paintbrush. Even with everything else going on this week, I still added to my collection. Because that's what it *means* to be in our club. It means finding treasures for your friends. Don't they want that too?

The igloo shudders in the wind. It bends, but it doesn't break. And suddenly, I hope it *does* storm. I hope the sky turns black and the trees shake and the storm sirens wail. I hope the igloo stays standing through it all.

Then they'll see. We built something strong but flexible.

And it can survive anything.

It never does storm on Saturday. The wind howls outside my window after I go to bed, but by the time I wake up on Sunday, there's nothing but a cold, steady rain outside.

I head downstairs, checking for any trip wires Dad might have set up to drop water balloons or shoot confetti cannons. When I get to the kitchen, he's standing with his back to me. He must have run in the rain, because he's soaking wet and chugging from a sports bottle.

But he doesn't hear me.

I hold my breath and creep closer, stepping over the creaky spot in the floor. When I'm right behind him, I throw out my arms and yell as loud as I can. "BOO!"

Dad sputters. He turns around, coughing at first, then laughing.

I lift my walkie-talkie from the charger and press the talk button. "Got you again, Zee Money," I say. "Over."

He picks up the other handset. "Again with the jump scare. Can't beat the classics, Big Zee. I'd better watch my back door, over."

"Roger that, over and out." I set down my walkie-talkie again. "What's for breakfast?"

"Just cereal." He takes out the Rainbow Pops, pours me a bowl, and moves toward the refrigerator.

"I'll get my own milk," I say, hurrying in front of him.

He raises an eyebrow. "Don't you trust me?"

"Nope."

He smirks and sets my bowl on the table.

I haul the jug over and pour the milk . . . then watch it turn *pink* in the bowl!

"How did you do that?" I demand.

Dad leans against the counter. "Drop of red food coloring at the bottom."

"I watched you pour the cereal!"

"But I've had the *bowl* ready for days." He starts peeling a banana. "You have to get up pretty early in the morning to outsmart old Zee Money."

I roll my eyes and sit down.

SNAP!

I jump back up. There's nothing on my seat, but when I lift the cushion, there's a sheet of bubble wrap underneath.

"Pretty early in the morning," Dad says again.

"Yeah, yeah," I say, grabbing my pill. "Was

Zee Money up early enough to go to the store?"

"He was indeed." He reaches on top of the refrigerator and brings me a plastic container of donut holes.

Yes! I pop it open and stuff one into my mouth.

"I thought those were for your prank," he says.

"What prank?" asks Rosie, shuffling into the kitchen.

I shoot Dad a look. "It's not a prank. It's a *project*." I hold up the container to show Rosie. "Ready?"

She squeals. "Yes, yes!"

We pull on our galoshes, grab our raincoats, and tumble out the door. Cold water splatters my legs as we run across the grass. While Rosie starts making a trench in the mud, I check around the yard for Oriol—in the bushes, behind the shed. I even peek under the tarp. Oriol might be just a cat, but I hope he found someplace dry to wait out the rain.

By the time I get back to the garden, Rosie is dropping donut holes into the ground. She sneaks a couple into her mouth.

"Don't eat all the seeds," I say.

She hands me the last one.

"So what kind of donuts should we grow?" I ask.

She tilts her head at me, her hair damp and curling around the edge of her hood. "What kind?"

"Yeah, powdered sugar, cinnamon—"

"Oh! Chocolate," she says.

"You got it." I run to the kitchen and come back with a bottle of chocolate syrup. I squeeze a line right on top of the donut holes and give Rosie a squirt. Then I take a swig myself while she covers the donut holes with mud.

"How many Sundays are left?" she asks as we move the wooden skewers to our new row.

"Just one after this."

"Can we plant the chicken feed next?"

"We talked about that."

"Please? We could give the chicks to Eli. That way we wouldn't have to eat them. And we could go visit!"

I shift on my feet. "Who says he'd even want them?"

She smiles. "He'd want them."

"Okay, fine, but he might not have room. He already wants to get rid of our igloo just to make space for a dumb rabbit hutch."

"Our chicks could live in his coop," Rosie says.

"But what if we accidentally grow a rooster?" I say. "It would wake up the whole neighborhood! Or what if—"

A loud clanging sound comes from the garage. Rosie and I look at each other then run to check it out.

Mom is kneeling on the cement floor, surrounded by metal rings. "Nothing to see here," she says. "I just knocked over my socket set."

"I'll get it," Rosie says. It looks like there are about a million pieces to slot back into the case, but she loves putting things into their exact-right places. She plops down and starts picking them up.

Mom ruffles her hair. "Thanks, sweetie."

I take another swig of chocolate syrup as I look around. The garage looks even worse than it did before Mom started cleaning in here. There's stuff everywhere. A stack of empty bins is piling up in the corner while cardboard boxes marked *donate* and *recycle* are starting to overflow.

At least that wonderful garage smell is stronger in the rain. I stick the chocolate syrup in my pocket and take a deep breath of must, metal, and concrete. Then I shrug off my raincoat and hang it on a tomato cage to drip-dry.

Mom lifts a plastic storage bin from the shelf. She sets it down and settles in next to it. Then she opens the lid and holds up a tiny yellow T-shirt with snaps at the bottom.

"What's that?" I ask.

"It's a onesie. You and your sister wore it when you were babies."

Huh. I guess baby clothes are named for your age. The shirts I wear now must be called *nine*sies.

Mom sets it in the cardboard box marked *donate*.

"Hang on," I say. "You're getting rid of it?"

"I was planning to."

"But you said it was mine. What if I want it?"

"What for?"

"I don't know." I grab it out of the box and spot a pyramid of plastic rings. "Were these mine too?" I ask, lifting them out.

"Yours and Rosie's."

The rings are stacked biggest to smallest, but they're in reverse rainbow order, purple to red. I dump them off the post and restack them, red to purple.

Mom chuckles. "You always made your sister stack them that way too."

"I did?"

"Yep."

I glance at Rosie, still organizing in the corner. I don't remember that. I start rummaging in the box. There are plastic cups that nestle inside each other, a yellow duck on wheels, a silver rattle that makes a tinkling sound when I shake it. Some of it seems familiar, but I'm not sure. "Why are you giving all this away?" I ask.

"Neither one of you has played with any of it in years."

"But what if I still want to?"

Mom lowers a tiny pair of snow boots. "Do you?"

"I mean, not right now. But . . . I don't know. Maybe someday." I spot a bag of our old refrigerator magnets shaped like letters. "You can't get rid of these," I cry, holding them up.

"I think you've got a pretty good handle on your alphabet."

"But I remember them!"

"Look, kiddo." Mom tosses the boots into the *donate* box. "These things aren't doing any good stashed in our garage. It's time to let someone else use them."

I scowl at the box. It's full of toys and books and clothes. The box marked *recycle* is full of—

I gasp and pull out a construction paper turkey.

No.

My heart beats faster as I rifle through drawings and finger paintings and homemade cards. I hold up a paper flower with my name on the back. "I *made* this!"

Mom gives me a guilty look.

"Do you throw away everything I make?"

Her face softens. "Of course not, honey. But I can't save everything, either."

"Why not?"

She pushes the plastic bin aside and waves me over. I sit on the floor in front of her. "Did I ever tell you about my great-aunt Mary?" she asks.

I shake my head.

"Aunt Mary loved quilting. She even had a whole room in her house for making quilts."

"Like my workshop?"

"Exactly like that." Mom tucks my hair behind my ear. "Her quilts were wonderful, too. When I was little, she made me a blue one that was covered in butterflies."

I know the one she's talking about. It's at the foot of her bed.

"But as she got older," Mom continues, "Aunt Mary stopped making quilts. She kept saying she wanted to get back to it, but . . ." Mom sighs. "When I was a teenager, we helped her move in with her sister, and do you know what we found?"

I imagine all the things you could find in an old person's house: a time machine, a closet that leads to Narnia, all those walnuts they put in their cookies. "What?"

"We found margarine tubs, stacked floor to ceiling in her quilting room."

"What's margarine?"

"Oh." She blinks at me. "It's fake butter. She used it for baking. And every time she finished a container, she washed and saved it, just in case."

"In case of what?"

"I don't know, honey. I don't think *she* knew.

She couldn't bear to throw them away. But she couldn't use them, either. And they ended up filling the space that she *could* have used for something she loved."

I look around. "Are you planning to make quilts in here?"

Mom smiles. "The point is, it's hard to let go. But it makes space for other things we care about. Maybe even things we haven't thought of yet. You see what I mean?"

I'm trying to. But the truth is, my brain is kind of busy thinking about what I could do with a jillion margarine tubs.

Mom rubs the tops of my arms. "Now, I have more sorting to do, and I don't think you should stay to watch."

"But—"

"Besides," she says, "you still have a workshop to clean. And this time . . ." She gives me a knowing look. "Some of that stuff has to actually leave the house."

I drag my feet all the way upstairs. I am *not* in the mood to clean. But if Present Meena doesn't do it, then Future Meena will be mad at Past Meena for putting it off.

I might as well get it over with.

But when I see the piles of treasures heaped against the walls of my workshop, I feel a twinge in my stomach. How can Mom expect me to part with any of this stuff? Sofía hasn't even decided what to make our new clubhouse out of yet. What if we need it?

Or what if it needs me?

Because here's the thing about collecting trash—the thing nobody knows.

Sometimes I think it *minds* being trash.

I mean, how would you feel if somebody tossed *you* out? How would you feel if you'd been a perfectly good *something* for a while, and then everyone decided you were good for *nothing*?

You'd feel surprised and hurt, that's how.

You'd wonder what you did to deserve it. You'd worry that nobody would ever want you again.

That's where I come in. I collect trash so it knows that somebody *does* want it. I give it a home. Another chance.

I rescue it.

And if I don't? Some of it will get recycled. Bottles and cans will get turned into bottles and cans again, shiny and perfect and new. Plastic might get a chance to be something else, like a T-shirt or a park bench.

But what about the trash? What about the corks and bottle caps and candy wrappers? If I get rid of them, they'll just go to the dump like they don't even matter. They'll end up at the bottom of a rotting heap of diapers and apple peels, wondering why nobody's coming for them.

And worst of all, no one will ever think of them again. Once something's in the trash, people act like it's gone forever.

But it *isn't*.

Every straw, every twist tie, every Styrofoam cup you've ever used is out there somewhere in a hulking, stinking heap of garbage.

Where are Aunt Mary's margarine tubs now, huh?

I bet I could have used them somehow, for something. I think they would have liked that.

I'll use all this stuff when I get a chance. As soon as we find Oriol, and Sofía is finally ready to work on our clubhouse, we'll come up with a plan together.

Until then, I need to hold on to anything we might want to use. But if some of it has to leave the house, like Mom says . . .

Fine.

I'll load it into my wagon and take it to Sofía's! At least then it'll look a little cleaner in here. And maybe Mom will leave me alone about quilting rooms and margarine and how space is better than stuff.

Now what can I pack up first?

I grab a plastic bag full of school lunch trash.

Phew! I yank it away from my face. Something in there *stinks*! I whip it across the room. A few pudding cups spill out when it lands.

I guess I could pack up my milk jugs instead. They're piled in a corner between gum wrappers and deflated balloons. I start stuffing them into a garbage bag and—

Holy ham balls, there's my supersuit! I haven't worn this baby in a while. I pull on the trash-bag tunic and strap on the swim mask. Then I pick up the plastic tablecloth I use for a cape and—

Raymond!

I dive for my rainbow-striped zebra. I haven't

seen him in *weeks*! I figured Dad hid him somewhere for a prank. I kept expecting him to turn up
in the refrigerator or at the bottom of the sandbox.
Was he here all along?

Geez, what else is hiding in these piles?

I hug Raymond tight and take a deep breath of
him that goes all the way through to his stuffing. I'll
have to tell Sofía I found him.

And I think I'll wear my suit.

It's still sprinkling when I tell Dad I'm headed to
Sofía's, but I don't wear my raincoat. My supersuit
will keep me dry enough.

It takes me a while to get there, though. First,
there are a lot of puddles to splash in. Second, I
can't let the earthworms drown while I'm dressed
like a superhero. I toss them into the grass, one by
one, and rinse my fingers off in the puddles. No
offense to nature, but I hate how the worms start
out gooshy and then curl up in a tight coil when
you touch them.

When I get to Sofía's, I don't bother to knock on
the door. I'm pretty sure I know where she is. Sure
enough, when I pull my wagon of jugs around back,
she's sitting on the stoop under a pink umbrella,
scrunched up small to keep from getting wet. She
must have heard my wheels squeaking, because she
looks like she's waiting for me.

"Hey," I say.

"Hi."

I gaze out into the yard. This place is the *best* when it rains. There's a low spot that fills up with so much water that it's like our own private lake.

Sometimes, when it's warm out, her mom even lets us swim in it. Other times, when it's too cold, we race leaves across the water instead.

I pick up a stick and toss it into the puddle. "Any sign of Oriol?" I ask.

She shakes her head and sighs. "He'd be too scared to come out in this."

"How do you know?"

"Because he sits by the door and howls whenever it rains."

I stand still for a minute and listen. I don't hear anything but the raindrops patting against my supersuit and hitting the ground all around us. If Oriol is howling somewhere, he must be too far away for us to hear. Or did something happen to him, and he can't make a sound?

I can tell from the crinkle in her forehead that Sofía is wondering the same thing.

"Maybe he's inside somewhere," I say, hoping to make her feel better. "Maybe he's warm and dry with a different family, like Eli said."

Sofía's frown deepens.

I pick up another stick and throw it at the water. It makes a nice plunk when it lands. "I bet he found *someone* to let him in," I say. "Oriol's a smart cat, even if he isn't the softest or the cutest."

She stares at me. "Who says he isn't the cutest?"

Uh-oh.

"Of all the cats in the whole wide world?" I scratch the front of my neck. "I mean, that doesn't seem very likely."

She presses her lips together and looks away.

I think I'd better change the subject. "See any interesting birds today?"

"There's a gull over there," she says in a flat voice, pointing.

I look across the water. My swim mask is fogging up, but when I push it to the top of my head, I see a white bird with gray streaks fluttering its wings at the edge of the giant puddle.

"I don't know what kind it is, though," Sofía says.

"There's more than one kind?"

"Yeah. Some like lakes. Some stay by the ocean." She shrugs. "You know."

We watch him poke his beak into the water. "I guess he thinks he's home," I say, tossing another stick.

Sofía gazes at me for a moment. Then she glances at the wagon behind me. "What's all that?"

"Milk jugs." I plop down on the stoop next to her. She shrinks away from my wet supersuit. When the rain stops hitting my head, I can hear it beating against the umbrella. "I had an idea."

She gives me a suspicious look. "What?"

"Mom is making me clean my workshop, but

there's nothing I can get rid of, so I thought I'd keep some of it here."

She blinks fast, then looks toward the water again.

"I mean, it's all stuff we might use for our new clubhouse anyway, so I figure it's at least half yours."

She starts twirling the umbrella above us. Drops fly off the little spokes. She moves her jaw back and forth, but she doesn't answer.

I get a funny feeling in my stomach. "You don't mind, do you?"

"No," she says quietly. "I don't mind."

"Okay, good." I relax and look around. "Where should I put them? The shed maybe?"

She shakes her head.

I rub the back of my neck. "How about I stuff them under your bed? Ooo, or what about that closet we used to play in? Do you think your mom would mind if we moved all the extra shoes?"

She takes a deep breath. "You can't keep it here."

I blink at her. "You said you didn't mind."

"I don't. I mean, I wouldn't. It's just . . ."

"What?"

She bites her lip. "We won't be here."

I feel a jolt in my body like lightning and scoot away from her. Outside the umbrella, rain starts to hammer against my head again. It seeps into my suit and trickles cold down my back. Even though it's only sprinkling out, my ears are starting to roar like they're full of thunder.

Sofía looks back at the vast puddle that isn't a lake. I follow her gaze to see the mixed-up gull spread his wings and fly away.

"Where are you going?" I ask, my heart pounding in my throat. My head is wet. My mouth is dry. And my voice is so tight and quiet that I'm not even sure she hears me.

But then she whispers, "California."

No. No, no, no!

"We're moving back to California."

I wheel my milk jugs back home in the rain. I steer around the earthworms, but I don't stop to pick any up this time.

They'll just have to fend for themselves.

The big blue tarp is lumpier than ever after I stuff the bag of jugs underneath.

At dinner, Dad sets a mini pizza in front of me. It's topped with Rainbow Pops, but I don't even smile when I see them. I just pick them off while Sofía's voice screeches in my head like the wagon: *We're moving back to California.*

I can't make myself say her words out loud. I clutch them like pennies I'm afraid to lose. I'm still gripping them that night when it stops raining, and I trudge out to the garden. And later, when I lie in bed, my chest squeezes around them so tightly that I can hardly breathe.

Mom says things always look brighter in the morning, though. I wake up on Monday *bursting* with new job ideas for Sofía's dad. I grab my necklace and race to my workshop.

A stench hits me when I open the door. It's like peeking into a trash bin that's been sitting in the sun. I pinch my nose as I breathe Magic Mist on the window and stare at the circle of fog. A week ago, I had so many wishes that I didn't know which one to pick.

Now I do.

I trace a square house with a triangle roof. I add windows, a door, and a curlicue of smoke rising from a chimney. I make a thumbprint in the middle of the square, imagining that it's Sofía, sitting inside the house. Then I close my eyes and make my wish: *I want her home.*

"Something stinks!"

Rosie is making a face in the doorway. I shoo her out and pull the door closed behind us. "What do you want?"

She lights up. "It's time to pick the donuts!"

In spite of everything, I get excited as we hurry across the yard. Rosie squeals when she sees the donuts, their icing gleaming in the sun. "You got your wish," I say. "Chocolate!"

She slides one off the stick. But when she turns it over, her smile fades. She picks another one and checks both sides. "Where are the sprinkles?" she asks.

I grab a donut and take a bite. "What sprinkles?"

She points at the dirt.

At first, I don't see anything. But when I peer closer, I spot tiny flecks of color dotting the ground. "Did you do that?" I ask.

She nods. "When you went to Sofía's yesterday."

"But I didn't know— I mean, I didn't have a chance . . ." I slide my Rainbow Ring back and forth on its string. "You didn't bury them," I say finally. "So they didn't grow roots."

Rosie tilts her head and squints at me. *Really?*

Something in her voice makes the bottoms of my feet tingle. "Don't you believe me?"

She doesn't answer, just looks at me very carefully.

I puff my chest out and put my hands on my hips. "Rosalyn Zee, have I ever lied to you?"

For a minute, it's like we're having a staring contest. I cross my fingers on both hands, but I'm not sure if I'm making a wish or telling a lie.

Both, I guess.

Finally, she drops her eyes and starts gathering donuts without a word.

I cram the rest of the donut into my mouth, checking for that twinge I get in my stomach when I'm doing something wrong. But Rosie loves the Magic Garden. Even if it isn't real, I'm doing it to be *nice*.

So why is it starting to feel like a mean prank?

★ ★ ★

The donut is still sitting in the pit of my stomach while I wait for Sofía in the tube slide before school. As soon as she climbs in, I blurt out, "Why doesn't he get some other job so you don't have to move?"

She blinks at me. "My dad?"

"Yeah. If he doesn't want to work on a different farm, he could still be a trucker. Or maybe a scuba diver!"

She smiles. "He'd need an ocean for that."

Shoot. "Then how about a magician's helper? I know that's usually a lady, but it's about time some boy got sawed in half."

She hesitates. "It's not just the job. He wants to be with family."

"But he's with you and your mom."

"That's not our *whole* family. It's hard being so far away. My cousins are like my brothers and sisters. And my aunts and uncles are like my other moms and dads."

I stare at her. I don't get that. I like my aunt Kathy and all, but she's not my *mom.*

"Anyway," Sofía says, "my dad brought us here for work, but I think the family always expected us to come back."

"But why do they get a say?"

She squints at me. "Because they're family."

"My grandparents moved to Florida when

they retired. They didn't give *us* a say."

Sofía gives me a strange look. "They went to live with strangers?"

I shrug. "They made friends."

She shakes her head. "That's not the same."

Anger flares in my chest. "But *we're* friends. Aren't *we* like family?"

She looks at her hands.

Wait a second.

I feel a chill on the back of my neck. "That's it," I say. I'm so excited that my voice doesn't work for a minute. I hold my idea like a baby bird, afraid to get too excited and crush it. "Let's be family," I whisper.

Sofía's eyebrows shoot up.

"So what if your mom and dad leave? *You* could stay." I can't get the words out fast enough. "Move in with us."

Her eyes widen. "Where would I sleep?"

"You can have my bed. Or I'll build you an igloo out back. Or take my workshop! I'll move all my stuff out, and you can hang your own art and draw wishes in the Magic Mist. You can even invite me in on Fridays, and we'll have sleepovers there like always."

"You'd get rid of your supplies?"

"I will if you stay!" And just like that, I get what Mom meant about making space for the things you care about. I loop my pinky through her friendship bracelet. "We'll be sisters," I say. "You and Rosie and me."

Sofía looks teary now, but in that way grown-ups get when they're happy. "I'd like to be your sister," she says.

My whole body feels like it's smiling now — even my elbows, even my knees!

And I know ... being sisters isn't all rainbows and lollipops. Sometimes sisters get on your nerves. Sometimes they ask too many questions about the tricks you play on them — even ones you play to be nice.

But you can't stop being family, not like you can stop being friends.

I hug myself and lie back in the slide. I'll make her a Rainbow Ring necklace, like Rosie's and mine. Sofía will have to take turns washing dishes, because that's only fair. We can stop serving cheese on taco night too, since she always said we're not supposed to. I feel a spark of jealousy at the thought of sharing Mom and Dad with her, but that just makes it seem like we're sisters already.

I start to wriggle out of the slide. "You wanna play four square, sis?"

"Meena, wait."

"Yeah?"

She doesn't say anything. She just traces her

thumbnail along the seam where two hunks of the plastic slide meet. She's quiet for so long that I'm afraid the bell will ring before we get a chance to play.

Finally, she says in a small voice, "I have to go with my mom and dad."

I stare at her. "But they could come and see you anytime. Or you could go to California to visit, like you do now."

She looks hard at me. "Would you leave your parents? Or Rosie?"

I suck in a breath.

I think of Mom tucking my hair behind my ear and Dad slipping bubble wrap onto my seat. I think of Rosie, looking up at me like I've never lied to her and never will.

And all at once, it starts sinking in—getting under my toenails and behind my eyeballs, shimmying down to the ends of my hair.

Sofía could leave.

She could move to California and never come back. She could fall into an earthquake crack or get crushed by the world's tallest tree. All because her dad refuses to be an acrobat.

I brace my arms against the sides of the tube. "You have to *do* something," I say. "Tell your parents you don't want to go. Tell them you hate it there!"

Sofía pulls back. "I don't hate it there. I like it."

"Better than you like it here?"

"You'd like it too," she says quickly. "Elena and I make up dances, and my little cousins always want us to chase them. My dad plays in my uncle's band, and my mom has way more people to talk to. She laughs all the time there. And every time we visit, I always wish we could stay longer."

I can't believe my ears. "Do you *want* to move?" I ask.

She bites her lip. "I'm just saying it won't be all bad."

I tumble out of the slide, feeling like I'm sinking in quicksand. *Of course it will be all bad,* my insides are screaming. *You'll be gone!* But the more I struggle, the faster I sink, so I hold the words inside so tightly that I start to shake.

I thought we were a pair of chickadees. I thought we were partner birds—that we'd always be together.

But what if Sofía is part of a flock? What if she's a sparrow, and I never knew it?

I think about how quiet she is whenever she gets back from California. For a few days after she visits, I have to talk a little softer and move a little slower until she perks back up and seems like herself again—or like the self I'm used to.

I thought her family there was like a dream

she had that I wasn't in. I thought it didn't matter. *Here* was real.

But all along, *there* mattered too. It mattered to her, and I never knew it.

What kind of friend *am* I?

"The only thing is . . . ," I hear Sofía say.

And even though I feel like I'm still sinking, when I turn and see the tears in her eyes, it's like I'm grabbing hold of a rope.

She doesn't want to fly away! She wants to stay here with me! I kneel down in the wood chips. "Yeah?"

She lets out a moan. "What if we can't find Oriol before we leave?"

I sit back on my heels. *Oriol?*

She's worried about leaving her cat? *He* never made her a valentine or a friendship bracelet. He never let her pick a project or hug his favorite stuffed animal when she was sad. What did he ever do but leave fur on her bed and scare away the birds she loves?

But when Sofía buries her face in her hands, I get up and dig my feet into the wood chips. "We're not done looking for him," I say.

When the bell rings, we walk toward the door. My shoulders feel stiff, and my heart is aching. But I grit my teeth and swallow down my hurt.

I promised to find her cat. A good friend keeps her promise.

And I'm *going* to be a good one if it's the last thing I do.

Which it might be.

Because I'm running out of time.

By lunchtime, everyone knows about Sofía. When I circle the tables to collect trash, Eli seems stunned. Maddy looks like she feels sorry for me. Lin drops an empty milk carton into my bag and blurts out, "I guess you'll be by yourself now."

I stare at all the stuff I collected. What am I saving this junk for anyway? Sofía is leaving. We'll never do our project together. I carry the whole bag to the garbage can. *Nobody wants you,* I think, stuffing it into the sludgy mess of goulash and fruit cocktail. *See how you like it.*

When school is over, Eli is waiting for me at the bike rack. He takes the lock off his front tire without looking at me. "She's really leaving?" he asks quietly.

I grab the handle of my empty wagon and nod, gritting my teeth against the rising hurt. He gets on his bike and starts pushing it beneath him while I walk alongside. "I promised we'd still find Oriol," I say.

Eli shoots me a worried look.

"What?"

"What if he doesn't want to be found?" he says.

"Why wouldn't he?"

Eli shrugs. "Maybe he went someplace he likes better."

I feel my face getting hot. "Or maybe some-body took him away and he didn't have a *choice*," I snap. "Maybe he even thought he'd like it, but now he's *stuck* there."

Eli holds up his hands. "Okay, geez!"

I scuff my foot against the sidewalk. "Stupid cat."

He stops his bike. "What's your deal with him, anyway?"

I look up. "What deal?"

"You never liked my pets very much, but you especially never liked Oriol."

I stare at him. "You could tell?"

"It's kinda obvious."

I frown. "Well, why should I like him? He never came when I called or fetched anything I threw. I even tried to teach him to roll over, but he just kept walking away."

Eli shakes his head. "Cats don't do any of those things."

I cross my arms. "Then I don't know why Sofía thinks he's so great."

Because he's like her, I realize suddenly. He's clean and quiet and understands Spanish. He likes birds but hates the rain. I'm not anything like that. I'm messy and loud, and I love to get wet. I think birds are boring, and I didn't even know Oriol was Spanish for oriole!

Is that why he's the only one of us Sofía is sorry to leave?

Well, I'll *make* her sorry. I'll find her dumb cat, and *then* we'll see which one of us she cares about.

"Hey, have you read anything good in your cat book?" I ask. "Anything that'll help us find Oriol?"

"I learned that cats have an extra eyelid," Eli says.

I scrunch up my nose. "Is that all?"

"And a group of cats is called a clowder."

"Anything else?"

"It turns out cats aren't supposed to drink milk. Everyone thinks they like it, but it's actually bad for their tummies."

I sigh. None of that will help. "What are we gonna do?" I say. "We've got kids all over town looking, but nobody's seen him."

"Too bad he doesn't have a bell on his collar," Eli says. "Maybe then they'd hear him, even if he's staying out of sight."

I think about that. "I wish we could rig up an alarm for him. Like when you get too close to a car, and it starts honking. Or when you brush against a case of diamonds, and all of a sudden there are lights flashing and sirens blaring and police running in." I chew the inside of my cheek. "We need something like that."

Eli kicks one of his pedals and makes it spin. "I wish I hadn't chased him away."

"It's not your fault he sounds like a squirrel."

I stop walking.

An Inspiration starts to tingle in the back of my mind. I think of the last time we saw Oriol, under Eli's feeder, *ack-ack-ack*ing at the birds. "Oriol could be the alarm," I breathe.

Eli turns to look at me. "What?"

"Remember that sound he made in your yard? We heard him all the way from the porch!"

"So?"

"So we get him to chirp like that. We get him to come out of hiding and make that noise so kids will hear him, even if they aren't looking."

"How do we get him to chirp like that?"

"We put up bird feeders." I can picture them perfectly. "We hang them all over. To attract the birds. To attract *Oriol*. We give him something to chatter at so he'll give himself away!"

Eli squeezes his handbrakes and lets them

go. "But where are we gonna get a bunch of bird feeders?"

I feel a slow smile spreading across my lips. "We're going to make them."

I'm so excited to get started that I run the rest of the way home. The wagon squeals behind me, but it's light and fast when it's empty, and it doesn't slow me down a bit.

As soon as I get there, I wheel around back and check the sandbox. Rosie must be inside, so I head straight for the big blue tarp to fetch my stash of jugs. I lift up the corner, and—

"What are you doing?"

I jump back.

Mom is hunched over her spinach bed in a sunhat and work gloves, watching me.

I clasp my hands behind me. "Just checking the dirt."

"Checking it for what?"

I rock back on my heels and think fast. "For earthworms," I say, crossing my fingers. "I thought you might want some. Eli says they're good for gardens."

She squints at me. "I'm good, thanks."

"Okay, then." I rub the back of my neck and take a few steps toward the house. "Well, if you change your mind—"

"Hold on."

I freeze.

Mom stands up and wipes the back of her glove across her cheek. She peers hard at me, and for a minute I feel like her crosswords probably do when she's trying to figure them out. Her gaze drifts over to the tarp.

Uh-oh.

I take another few steps toward the house as she strides toward the dirt pile, lifts the corner of the tarp, and gasps.

She whisks back the plastic to reveal my whole stash of garbage—the flowerpots, the rocking chair, the bicycle tires . . . everything I saved.

"Wow, where did that come from?" I ask.

Mom whips her head around. "You tell me."

"Oh, well . . ." I scratch the front of my neck. "I guess I found it on the curb?"

She puts her hands on her hips. "Whose curb?"

I grind my sneaker into the grass. "Ours."

Her voice goes up a notch. "You dragged this back here after I got *rid* of it?"

"You never said not to."

She covers her eyes with her gloved hands. She takes a big breath in . . . and lets it out. Then she lowers her arms and looks right at me. "Get it out of here."

"Why? It's not bothering anyone."

"Because I don't want it here, Meena! Our

yard is not a landfill, and it's not a recycling center. And hiding it from me is *lying*." She yanks off her gloves. "Now take this stuff back to the curb, where it belongs, and don't make me tell you again."

"But I might need it someday," I say, pleading now.

She gives me a warning look, her eyes so fierce that I clamp my mouth shut.

I don't know how many trips it takes to wheel everything around front—the dresser drawers, the lawn chair, the couch cushions. Mom stands with her arms crossed and watches me haul everything to the curb, one load at a time. When I'm finished, she even takes a shovel and jabs the dirt pile a few times to make sure there's nothing buried in it.

I'm not gonna lie. I kind of wish I'd thought of that.

Finally, she sends me inside.

Rosie is watching her dragon show in the living room, Pink Pony by her side. I wander over to the window and stare out at all those wonderful treasures lined up on the curb.

So what if I love it? I ask myself. *I wasn't using it. I don't need it.*

But I'm only lying to myself now.

I do need it—at least some of it.

So I slip outside, grab my bag of milk jugs out of the recycling bin, and race upstairs.

13

The smell in my workshop is starting to leak into the hallway.

I slam the door behind me and heave open a window. It doesn't help much, but I have work to do, so I pull my shirt up over my nose and dump out the jugs.

What should I make first?

I cut holes in the sides and tie strings to the handles while my brain gets busy with ideas. There are so many different kinds of bird feeders I could make! The birds probably don't care, as long as they're full of food, but more people might hang them if they like the way they look.

I think about the kids in my class. Lin likes outer space, so I cover one in tinfoil and make it look like a rocket. Aiden is crazy about sweets, so I scrape the bottom of my valentine box for candy hearts and glue them all over another jug. Pedro is into sports, so I cover a feeder with doodles of kickballs and basketball hoops.

On Tuesday, I nestle the jugs into my wagon and cart them to school. When I drop off Rosie at the front door, Eli is waiting. "What are those?" I ask as he tosses a baggie into each jug.

"Sunflower seeds."

"Oh. Sofía put oatmeal in hers."

"That's good too." He grabs the straps of his backpack and frowns. "Are you sure about this? I don't like Oriol hunting the birds."

"Sofía says he never catches them," I say. "But he has to try, or we'll never hear him."

Eli nods, but he still looks worried.

I pull my wagon to the middle of the play-ground and park it. Then I clear my throat and cup my hands around my mouth. "Hear ye, hear ye," I shout. "Step right up!"

Maddy and Nora stop jumping rope. Pedro stops bouncing his basketball. A group of first grad-ers stops playing tag. I nod to Eli.

"Ack-ack-ack!" He makes the squirrel sound in the back of his throat. *"Ack-ack-ack!"*

I turn to the kids who are wandering over. "That's what you'll hear if you're the lucky one who brings our lost kitty home."

Lin kicks the wheel of my wagon. "What are those? Bird feeders?"

I spread my arms wide. "They're cat detectors."

"They look like bird feeders."

I spot Sofía, pressing up to the back of the crowd. "They're super-duper, *one-of-a-kind* bird feeders," I say, "specially designed to detect lost kitties. A certain lost kitty, that is. Anyone who takes one of these babies home is guaranteed to attract birds, which will attract Oriol, and *whamo*! That's how we'll find him."

"What's the reward?" Aiden asks.

I lower my arms. "Reward?"

"Yeah. What do we get if we catch the cat?"

"You don't need a reward," I say in a booming voice.

"I'd take gummy worms," Aiden says.

I look at Eli. He shrugs. I hand Aiden the superhero jug. "Then gummy worms you shall have!"

"Just hang them somewhere you'll be able to hear him," Eli says as we start passing out feeders. "And put them up high enough that Oriol won't be able to reach the birds."

Sofía waits until the end of the line. "You made those for Oriol?" she asks me, her eyes shining.

I nod. "What are friends for?"

She picks up the last jug, holds it by the string, and watches it spin. I'm pretty proud of that one. I painted it forest green and glued twigs all over it. I'm hoping to trick the birds into thinking it's part of nature, like maybe a sunflower tree. Maybe they'll even want to build a nest inside and stay.

The Taylor twins run up. "Do you have any left?"

Sofía hands them the jug. As they walk away, she squeezes her eyes shut and crosses her fingers. "I hope this works!"

"I'll make more tonight," I tell her. "We'll have bird feeders hanging all over town in no time."

She grins. "I'd love that."

"Hey," I say, realizing something. "This was your idea."

"What was?"

I bump my shoulder against hers. "I wanted to do a project, but you were the one who picked bird feeders. And now we're making the birds a whole *city*!" I'm getting excited now. "You wanna come over and help me after school? This could be the best thing we ever made together!"

Her smile falters. She glances from me to Eli. "I'll ask, but I think Mom wants me to start packing."

I feel my shoulders sag. "Already?"

"When are you leaving?" Eli asks.

Sofía cringes. "Sunday."

I gasp. "*This* Sunday?"

She nods. "If we're not out by the end of April, we have to pay another month's rent."

We all stand there, stunned. I count the days in

my head. I count them again on my fingers, hoping I'm wrong.

But no matter how many times I count them, Sunday is only five days from now.

For the rest of the morning, my brain feels like a squishy gray blob. I'm supposed to be listening to directions about poetry and fractions, but I can't hear anything over my heart pounding in my ears. It drowns out the sounds of the lunchroom too. I feel like I'm underwater as I watch kids dump chip bags and yogurt sleeves into the trash.

When I get home, I set my walkie-talkie on the charger and check out back. Mom and Rosie are in the garden together, smiling and laughing. They don't even know about Sofía, I realize. And all of a sudden, I'm so jealous I could scream. I wish I didn't know she was leaving. I wish I could go back to thinking I had all the time in the world to play with her and talk to her and do nice things for her.

But I have only five days left. So I trudge up to my workshop to make more bird feeders before I'm out of time.

I stop at the top of the stairs. There's a different smell today—like mouthwash and lemons. It gets stronger the closer I get to my workshop. Then I push open the door.

The floor is empty, down to the speckled gray carpet.

Dad.

He got me again! I shake my head as I open the closet door, nice and slow, expecting all my supplies to come tumbling out like they do in cartoons when someone's crammed a bunch of stuff inside.

But they don't. There's nothing in there but some extra blankets.

I take a look around. Raymond is sitting on my spinny office chair in the middle of the room. A few crates of art supplies line the walls. It's just the stuff you buy at the store, though—markers and stickers, scissors and tape.

Where's the stuff I collected?

I check under the beds and in the other closets, my mind already sparking with ideas about how to get Dad back. I could hide all his left shoes or take the batteries out of the remotes. Or maybe I'll fill his water bottle with hot sauce!

"There you are," Mom says when I get back down to the kitchen.

"Do you know where Dad put my stuff?" I ask.

"What stuff?"

"From my workshop."

She yanks off her gardening gloves. "You mean the stuff I asked you to clean up? You mean the *trash* you were supposed to throw away?"

I stiffen. "It's not trash. It's supplies."

"Well, those *supplies* were reeking up the whole upstairs."

I get a sinking feeling in my stomach. "What did you do with them?"

She throws up her hands. "What do you think?"

I take a step back. *No.* Then I run outside and lift the lid of the recycling bin. *No, no, no!* It's full of flattened milk jugs.

"How could you do this?" I cry when Mom comes out.

"How could *you*? The room was full of garbage, Meena! Sour milk, moldy applesauce, rotting—"

"The milk jugs weren't garbage," I say. "They were recycling."

"Which you were supposed to sort. I asked you to *clean* your workshop, not fill it like a dumpster."

I grab a jug and try to press it back into shape. I push and pull on it. I try blowing it up like a balloon. Nothing works. I hold the crumpled jug in my hands, imagining Mom stomping down on it. It feels like my heart that's getting smashed inside my chest. "I needed these," I moan.

Mom rubs her forehead and lets out a big breath. "You always say that."

"I needed them to find Oriol," I cry. "Before Sofía moves away and never comes back!"

Mom lowers her hand. "What did you say?"

"She's moving back to California," I blurt out.
"On *Sunday*."

Mom stares at me. "Are you sure?"

"Of course I'm sure!"

And now I'll never find Oriol. And she'll never
know what a good friend I am. And she won't even
be sorry she left. She'll be so busy rollerblading
and dancing and playing chase that she'll forget all
about me, like something she threw away.

I slump against the bin.

But if I had enough jugs, my plan might have
worked. Maybe then Sofía would know I'm the kind
of friend she could never leave. Maybe she would
have even convinced her parents to stay. Because
no matter how great California is, she'd never go
anywhere I'm *not*.

I'd make bird feeders forever if it would keep
her here.

I stand up straight. I'll just have to use something else.

I turn and push over the bin. I hear Mom gasp
behind me as flattened milk jugs skitter across the
driveway. Bottles and cans and boxes spill out next.
I wade into the pile and start kicking things around,
looking for something I can use.

But the bottles are too small. The boxes aren't
rainproof. The cans are too hard to cut.

I toss my head back and cover my eyes, my

chest heaving. "I had what I needed."

"Meena—"

"I want what I *had*."

For a minute, I stand there shaking, holding the tears inside. When I feel Mom's hands on my shoulders, I pull away and head for the house.

"Where are you going?" she asks.

"To get some milk."

I storm into the kitchen. I feel her behind me, watching me open the refrigerator and empty the last of the milk into a glass. I chug it down then hug the empty jug to me and glare at her.

She gazes back with a look I've never seen before. Horrified. Unsure. I wait for her to tell me to go clean up the driveway, but instead she hooks a hand on the back of her neck and says, "Be sure to wash it out so it—"

"—doesn't stink. Yeah, yeah."

I rinse out the jug and shake out as many drips as I can. Then I turn it over in my hands.

One bird feeder. That's all I can make.

But I'm not making it here. I'm not doing anything in that clean, empty space upstairs that doesn't feel like mine.

"I'm going to Eli's," I say.

Then I stomp out the door, leaving my walkie-talkie behind.

14

"D o you have any milk?" I ask when Eli answers his door.

He doesn't even reply. He just leads the way to the kitchen, gets the milk from the fridge, and pours me a glass. I chug it down and motion for him to pour me another. "Mom got rid of my jugs," I say.

He pours himself some then. We sit there, downing milk in silence. By the time the jug is empty, my stomach is sloshy and achy and full. But I can still only make two feeders.

"We could ask kids at school," Eli says. "We'd get more jugs in a couple of days."

"We need them now." I let out a long breath. "You want to make a bird feeder?"

He shakes his head. "I'm gonna go spend time with Lizzy."

I'm not exactly sure how you can spend time with a fish, but I nod. "Is she okay?"

He looks away. "She won't be around much longer."

When he scuffs off to his room, I slip through the sliding door and onto the back porch.

The igloo is still blocked by yellow tape. It looks worse than ever—not like something could happen to it, like something already *did*. It doesn't seem strong and flexible. It seems fragile and shaky.

Everything does.

A few weeks ago, I had everything I wanted. A best friend. A clubhouse. A workshop full of treasures.

Now Sofía is leaving. My workshop is empty. And our igloo . . . I gaze at the plastic dome, listing to one side on top of the umbrella. Maybe Mom is right. You can't keep everything. But can't I keep the things I saved? The ones that matter most?

I give the igloo a gentle shove and watch it sag even farther to the left. I don't know how to fix it. I don't even know why I should. We'll never expand the club to new locations now. But when I think of all the weeks I spent dragging jugs here to make it—

I suck in a breath and stagger backward.

An Inspiration. That's what this is.

This time, though, it doesn't feel like a tingle in the back of my brain or the sun coming up in my chest.

It's a sharp jolt that almost knocks me over.

I rest my hand on the entrance, feeling the

smooth curve of the plastic beneath my fingers. *I'm sorry.* I hold the words inside my heart. *I'm so sorry.*

Then I grab a handle and pull.

When the jug breaks free, the tape makes a ripping sound. I feel it all the way down to my toes.

Our clubhouse looks unfinished now—like it will never be whole again.

But I have all the jugs I need.

Maybe this was what I was saving them for.

By the time I leave Eli's, there's a gaping hole in the ceiling of the igloo, and the doorway looks like a mouth that's missing some teeth.

But I have another batch of bird feeders.

Kids line up when they see me coming on Wednesday. I pass out all the jugs in no time. Sofía shows up with new fliers to go with them. *ACK-ACK-ACK*, they say across the top. They explain what to listen for and what to do if Oriol shows up. She gives me a big stack too, in case I pass out bird feeders to the neighbors.

But she never does come to help me make them.

Eli does. That afternoon, and again on Thursday, I head back to his house and sit in the igloo, ripping out one jug at a time. When he's done with his pets, he cuts the holes, ties strings to the handles, and tapes bags of birdseed inside. Then I decorate the jugs. I make each one as special as I can with scraps

of paper, markers, and tape. When we're finished, we load them into the wagon.

Every morning, I give away another batch. Kids report which birds they've seen. Eli tells their names—cardinals and finches and chickadees. Sofía points them out in her book. Kids talk about the squirrels they've spotted too, hanging from the feeders or walking down the strings like tightropes.

But nobody has seen Oriol.

On Friday, I pass out the last wagonload of jugs and sit on a bench to wait for Sofía. "Guess who," she says from behind. I turn to see her in a floaty white dress and shoes that buckle. "Why are you so fancy?" I ask.

She does a little twirl. "Mom said I could wear my Easter dress for my last day."

Her last day. I swallow hard and point to the container she's holding. "What's in there?"

She opens the lid to show me the cupcakes inside. "Birthday treats."

"It's not your birthday."

She closes the lid. "But I won't be here then."

I suck in a sharp breath. Her birthday. *My* birthday.

What else is she going to miss?

Lots of things, I realize. The day Eli gets his new rabbit. The day we clean our desktops with shaving cream. The day Rosie graduates from kindergarten in a cardboard hat. Our next year of school. Our next everything.

And then the bell rings, and we've missed our before-school playtime too—the last one we'll ever have.

I'm *not* missing anything else.

For the rest of the day, I'm on high alert, collecting every moment. I gather them in, store them up, and tuck them away for safekeeping.

The last time we say the Pledge of Allegiance, I notice that Sofía taps her pinky finger the whole time she has her hand over her heart. The last time she gives me the can tab off her apple juice, I notice how the pointy bits press into my palm. The last time we sit in the tube slide for recess, I notice how the orange plastic makes her cheeks glows like tangerines.

At the end of the day, Sofía passes out her cupcakes, and everybody makes good-bye cards for her. "Would you like to keep your clip?" Mrs. D asks her, taking the clothespin off our behavior chart. "Or would you rather leave it here to remind us of you?"

Sofía blushes. "Leave it here."

"Then I know right where it belongs." Mrs. D pins it to the top of the chart, next to At My Best. She winks at Sofía. "That's where it spent most of its time anyway."

I stare at my own clip. It's sitting at Ready for Anything.

But I'm not ready! There's so much more I want to do with Sofía. I want to make projects and have sleepovers and do our Friday playdates. I want to cheer her up when she's sad and root for her when she's nervous. I want to find Oriol, like I promised.

My eyes trail down the chart to Last Chance. That's where my clip should be.

When the bell rings, kids wave and shout to Sofía as they head into the hall. Mrs. D helps gather her supplies and gives her a hug. "We'll be thinking about you," she says. "Let me know if there's anything you need."

Sofía's backpack is so full that she looks like a floaty white turtle as we head down the hallway.

This is the last time we'll ever leave school together, I think. *This is our last Friday playdate.* We have to make the most of it—make it our best playdate yet. So when we step out of the building, I take a big breath of sunshine and smile. "Do you want to drop this stuff off at your house before you come over?"

She stops. "Oh," she says.

I blink. "Oh, what?"

"I can't come today. I meant to tell you."

I stare at her. "But it's Friday. We always play on Friday."

She toes the ground.

My throat swells. Last Friday, we stuck fliers into mailboxes and looked for Oriol. That was our last playdate, and I didn't even know it.

It's not fair! I want to kick and scream. I want to throw my backpack right here on the sidewalk. It's like someone stole my last bite of ice cream— the one I saved for the end. And if I'd *known* I was taking my last bite, I would have paid more attention. I would have let it melt in my mouth and savored it. But I can't go back and do it now, because it's already *gone*!

"What about tomorrow?" I ask, getting desperate. "Can you play then?"

"Maybe," she says, "but people from my church are coming to help load the van."

"Then how about we help too?" I ask quickly.

"My whole family can come. That way it'll go faster, and maybe there will be time left to play."

She nods. "Okay." She starts down the sidewalk and calls over her shoulder. "See you tomorrow!"

Then instead of walking together like we do every Friday—like I thought we always would—I watch her walk away, alone.

15

When Eli lets me in, I go straight to the back porch.

Our igloo looks like a big plastic horseshoe now, only two rows high. I plop down in the middle of it, rip a jug from the base, and start making another feeder.

I don't know why I bother. They haven't helped us find Oriol. And Sofía will be gone before I can take more to school. But I harvest the last of the jugs anyway, one by one. Whenever the wagon is full, Eli wheels it into the neighborhood. He leaves the feeders on doorsteps along with our new flier. Every time he heads out, he's gone longer, because he's taking them farther from home.

The jugs aren't even special anymore. I'm making them with my hands, not my heart. Sometimes I cover four or five in rainclouds before I remember to make something cheerful. But as long as I'm making feeders, I feel like I'm doing *something* for Sofía. So I just keep cranking them out like a factory as the igloo disappears around me.

Then I'm down to my last jug.

I take my time with it, paying attention to every detail. I cut the holes nice and even, feeling my scissors glide through the plastic. I tie the string with a bow, tight and pretty. Then I take my markers and cover it with rainbow stripes. This time, they're straight, and they go all the way around.

Finally, when there isn't a single jug left, I load up the wagon for the last time and peek into Eli's room. He's sitting next to the aquarium, reading his cat book out loud to Lizzy. I see her tail fin flick, but otherwise she's as still as ever. When Eli's voice reaches her through the water, it must sound muffled and warped.

But I guess this is all he can think of to do for her now.

On Saturday, my whole family heads to Sofía's.

Mom and Dad help load furniture into the moving van. The upstairs neighbor wraps dishes in newspaper. People are dusting shelves and taking down curtains, some chattering in English, some in Spanish. I wander around, peering into empty rooms and cupboards. Once in a while a grown-up calls for me to hold open a door, but I get the feeling they're just doing it to be nice.

I'm peeking into the hall closet when Rosie runs by with Sofía's bird feeder. "Where are you taking that?" I ask.

"To the moving van."

"You can't," I say. "It's for Oriol."

"But Mom said."

I feel my shoulders slumping. "Please put it back, Rosie. She's leaving tomorrow. Tonight's our last chance."

She gives me a sad look before heading back outside. When she's gone, I duck into the closet, slide the door closed, and sink to the floor. For a while, I rest my head on my knees, listening to the bustle outside. Sofía and I used to sit right here, sipping strawberry milk and eating sweet buns with pretty crisscross tops. Now she's leaving, and I haven't been able to stop it.

But you know what? She hasn't been much help either. All this time, I've been trying to be a good friend to her—the best friend I could be. But Sofía hasn't been doing so hot herself. She didn't collect anything for our club last week or help with the bird feeders. She skipped our last playdate. All she thinks about is Oriol.

And now she's in her room packing. She hasn't even come looking for me. It's supposed to be club day, but I doubt she remembers. We probably won't even *have* a club after she moves. The thought makes me feel as empty as the closet.

But the thought of missing our last day together feels worse. So I take a big breath, get to my feet, and go to find her.

She's taking things down from her wall. A sleeping bag is stretched out where her bed used to be. Her dresser is gone, but the drawers are against the wall, still full of clothes. There's a laundry bag at my feet with a fuzzy, purple leg sticking out of the top.

I know that leg. "Lobo!"

Sofía looks up as I pull out a stuffed puppy with big eyes and floppy ears.

"He was your favorite," I say. "You always ran to hug him as soon as you got home from school."

She smiles. "I forgot about that."

"When did you stop?"

She tilts her head to one side. "I guess when I got Oriol, I ran to hug him instead."

I feel the front of my neck getting hot. "I really thought we'd find him."

She bites her lip and turns back to the wall.

I set Lobo in the middle of her pillow in case she needs to hug someone later. "You always brought this guy to our sleepovers, too." I let out a big sigh. "I wish we could have had one more before you left."

She looks around again. "Why can't we?"

I perk up at that. "Would your parents let you?"

"I think so."

My heart does a swoop. "You have to pack a bag, then. Quick, before everything is on the truck!"

"Oh." Her face falls. "You want to do it at your house?"

I hesitate. "You want to do it here?"

She looks around at the half-empty room. "It's my last night."

My heart sinks again. "But then we'll never have another sleepover at my house."

"We might," she says. "If we come to visit."

If.

I look away. I should let her pick. But I *love* having Sofía sleep over at my house. We build forts in the backyard and tell funny stories and eat all our favorite snacks. We sleep on the floor of my workshop, surrounded by piles of treasures.

But those are gone now.

I sink down onto her sleeping bag. "We can have it here," I say quietly.

Sofía looks thoughtful. "How about we split it?"

"What do you mean?"

"How about we do all the *activities* at your house, then come back here for the actual sleeping?"

I spring back up. "Okay." I smooth out her sleeping bag and go to stand next to her. The wall is covered with artwork: colorful birds, smiling suns, and tissue paper flags with fancy designs cut into them. "Where do you want these?" I ask.

"I'm packing the ones I want to keep."

"What about the others?"

She shrugs. "Recycle them, I guess."

I look at the two piles on the floor next to her. One is neat and careful. The other is sort of a jumble. I spot a picture I drew of her on top.

Is she getting rid of that?

I turn back to the wall. I don't want to know if she is.

I start picking at a piece of tape. It's holding up a big sheet of newsprint—the first thing we ever made together, back in kindergarten. The paper is curling at the edges, but it's covered in colorful smears and splatters. They're the exact color of our first smile, our first laugh, our first day as friends.

I put my palm over an orange handprint. "Look how small our hands were!"

Sofía presses her own palm to the paper. "Mine is bigger than yours now."

"No, it isn't."

"Is too."

"Hang on," I say. Her craft supplies are in a crate by the door, so I grab the ink pads she uses for stamping, open the red one, and smear my hand across the sponge. Then I press my hand against the paper and make a new print. "Your turn," I say, handing her the purple ink.

She grins, smears her hand through the ink, and makes a purple print right next to mine. "Told you it's bigger," she says.

"But we didn't check our other hands!" We slather ourselves with ink again and make two more prints. "Okay, fine," I say. "But I bet my *feet* are bigger than yours." I start pulling off my sneaker.

She laughs and grabs the ink pad away from me. "You're not putting your feet in there!"

I grin up at her. I haven't heard Sofía laugh much lately, I realize. The sound reminds me of bubbles floating into the air above us. For a minute, my heart feels like it's hovering up there with them, turning and making rainbows in the light.

It still feels floaty when we wash our hands and get back to work. I take my time loosening all four corners of the newsprint with my thumbnail. It comes off the wall nice and clean. I'm careful to fold the tape so it doesn't get stuck on anything. Then I lay the painting gently across the *keep* pile.

"I'm not packing that one," Sofía says.

I blink at her. "You're not?"

"You can set it over there." She points to the other pile.

And just like that, I feel my heart bubble burst,

splattering inside me like the dried-up paint. I slide the poster over to the other stack of papers and take a long last look at those bright, mixed-together colors. Then I turn away from them and back to the wall.

16

The house is almost empty now.

Grown-ups stand talking in the driveway while Sofía's dad passes out bottles of brightly colored sodas. Mine is pineapple, so I should feel like I'm sipping on sunshine, but all the yellow gets sucked into the gray quicksand inside me.

Then Sofía talks to her dad, who talks to Mom, and soon, we're heading home for a sleepover— probably our last one ever.

There's lots of room in my workshop, and the lemon-over-garbage smell is almost gone. We spread blankets and pillows on the floor like always, even though we aren't sleeping here. We take our time making our own little pile of softness then sit facing each other, like two birds in separate nests.

I usually have a zillion ideas for our sleepovers, but my mind is as blank as the room. We can't do a project, since my treasures are gone. Sofía didn't bring any Duvalín to snack on, because somebody already packed it. She even left Lobo behind, so I feel like a baby holding Raymond in my lap, even though I really need something to hug. "What do you want to do?" I ask finally.

"We could make more bird feeders."

"I'm all out of jugs," I say. She'd know that if she ever came to help.

Her face falls. "Could we do something outside, then? In case Oriol . . . ?" Her eyes drift toward the window.

Anger swells in my chest. She's still thinking about him. Still! *I* made the bird feeders. I searched neighborhoods and took apart the best thing I ever made, all for her. All for a chance to find him, because that's what a good friend would do. I stayed by her side after Oriol *left*. But she's still thinking about him instead of me.

She wanders over to the window and looks out, her face so worried that I feel the anger shriveling up inside me.

I let out a breath. "I still have a wagonload of feeders," I say. "I ran out of houses to deliver them to. We could hang them here if you want."

The sun is low in the sky when we get to the backyard. The trees cast long shadows across the grass. We tie the rest of the jugs to low-hanging branches and scoop sunflower seeds into them all. When we're finished, I refill the jug by the garden with the crooked, rainbow-colored tape. Then we sit on the edge of the sandbox, the bird feeders swaying in the breeze like paper lanterns.

"Do you think the squirrels will eat all the seeds?" Sofía asks.

I shrug. What difference does it make? After tomorrow, she'll be gone, and I won't have any reason to look for Oriol.

Something above us whistles: *Yoo-hoo. Yoo-hoo.*

Sofía looks up. "Hey, little chickadee." I follow her gaze to a black-and-white bird, hopping along a branch. "Where's your friend?" she asks.

I spot a second bird higher up in the tree and point. "There."

For a while, we watch the chickadees swoop for the feeder, steal seeds, and carry them back to a branch to peck at them. Finally, they flit away, making funny, U-shaped dips in the air.

Sofía rests her elbows on her knees. "My dad said we wouldn't leave Oriol behind," she says. "Do you think he meant it?"

I remember what Mom said when she sent me to clean my workshop: *You can keep the things you love.* Now my treasures are gone. The igloo is too. I'm losing Sofía next. "I think parents say a lot of things that don't come true," I tell her. "Like *in a minute.* And *everything will be okay.*"

Sofía nods. "My mom keeps saying that. But

how can anything be okay if Oriol is missing?" She clenches her hands into fists. "I don't want to leave him."

I feel that like a punch in my stomach. She still isn't talking about me.

But at the same time, a tiny balloon of hope starts to fill up my chest. What if her parents *did* mean what they said? Maybe if they don't find Oriol, *they won't leave.*

The balloon turns hard and cold. In that case, I hope Oriol stays lost. I hope someone took him, or that he's trapped somewhere. I hope he's chasing rabbits he can never catch. I hope he's so lost that he can never find his way home.

I don't even *want* the bird feeders to work now. I want to go roaring across the grass and chop them right out of the trees. I want to smash every last jug under my feet.

But instead I cross my fingers and hope I never see Oriol again. "You should tell your parents," I say, desperate. "Tell them you won't leave without Oriol. He belongs to *you.*"

"Maybe." Sofía tips her face up to the sky. "But what if he belongs to himself?"

"What do you mean?"

She's quiet for a minute. "It was raining when we found him," she says finally. "Did I ever tell you that?"

I shake my head, still crossing my fingers so tightly they pinch.

"We heard him howling in the backyard. He was skinny and dirty, and his fur was matted down." She picks at the grass. "But when we opened the door, he came right in and curled up by the heat vent. It was like he already knew what it was. Like he'd lived in a house before."

I imagine a scrawny Oriol, licking mud off his paws.

"My dad called the animal shelter, but they never found an owner. But I can't stop thinking about what Eli said—about how maybe Oriol has another family. I've been so scared that he'd go back to them, and I'd never see him again. I sat on the back stoop all week so if he came, he'd know I was waiting. So maybe he'd pick me."

I sit up straighter. "If you stay, we can do that together. I'll wait with you every day." I picture us sitting on her back stoop—a week, a month, a year from now. I think of us crossing our fingers, making opposite wishes, like we are now.

"But the thing is," Sofía says quietly, "now I hope Oriol *does* have another family."

"What?" I turn to stare at her. "Why?"

"Because that would mean he's safe. It would mean he isn't lost at all. He's with people who love him. It would mean he's found his way home."

"But don't you want him back?"

Sofía takes a deep breath. "Not as much as I want him to be happy."

We're quiet for a while. I think of Oriol, clean and dry, curled up somewhere safe and warm. I feel the balloon in my chest softening, losing air.

"Do you think I'll ever see him again?" Sofía asks.

My shoulders slump. "I don't know."

She wraps her long hair around her finger. "I think I could let him go if I knew he was okay. It would hurt, but I could do it, you know?"

Do I know?

Could I let Sofía go? Do I want her to be okay, even if it's somewhere else? Do I want her to be safe and happy—to feel at home, even if it isn't with me?

I *want* to want that.

Across the yard, a flock of sparrows crowds around a feeder. It swings and spins as they cling to it.

"I just hope his other family knows he likes strawberries," Sofía says, "and that he's scared to jump down from the bed. I hope they know he won't hurt the birds, even if he tries to." She takes a shaky breath. "And I hope he doesn't forget me."

I jump up and whirl to face her. "He would

never. You were his best friend. He couldn't forget that. No matter where he is now. No matter who he's with."

Her eyes fill with tears.

My heart aches for her. I wish I could take all her sadness away. I wish I could fill her with color and light and cover her with rainbows. I wish someone could.

"Hey." I smack my hands against my thighs. "We're supposed to be having a sleepover here, right?"

She nods.

I swallow hard. "And if this is the last one we ever have, we should make it our *best* one. So pick something. Anything. A movie, a game, a project . . . whatever you want."

She tilts her head to one side. "Hide-and-seek?"

"You got it." I grab her hand and pull her up. "I'll hide, you seek. No basement, no garage, and no other yards. Go!"

She covers her eyes and starts counting. "One . . . two . . ."

I turn and race through the grass on tiptoe, weaving in and out of bird feeders without making a sound.

"Ten . . . eleven . . ."

I lift the corner of the blue tarp, scurry under it, and pull it over my head, like I'm tucking myself in.

"Nineteen . . . twenty!"

I hold my breath and peer through a metal ring in the tarp. Sofía looks in the bushes and behind the trees. She goes around the side of the house and reappears a minute later on the other side. I hold as still as I can, breathing the smell of plastic and dirt until I hear the back door open and close behind her.

I throw off the tarp and take a big breath of clean air. I guess Sofía just can't imagine hiding in a pile of dirt, because she's never found me here.

And now she never will, I realize.

I stare through the branches above me. Who will look for me if she leaves? Will it just be me, all by myself, with an empty workshop and a garden that isn't really magic and nothing but these bird feeders to remind me that she was ever here?

Something makes a clicking sound by the garden. I groan. At least I'll have the squirrels for company. It seems like you can't get rid of them, even if you want to. I hear the chattering again. Two chickadees flit away from the sound. I sit up to shoo the squirrel away.

I freeze.

A pair of yellow eyes stares back at me.

He looks pretty rough there under the jug. He's skinny and scruffy, and his tail is full of burrs. I start to get up, but when the tarp crinkles, his body tenses, and his eyes narrow to slits, like he's about to skitter off. So I stay still and make a clicking sound with my teeth.

His eyes widen.

I don't move. I don't even breathe. Then, very slowly, I reach out my hand and murmur the words I've heard so many times but don't understand. *"Michi, michi, michi. Aquí, gatito."*

He takes a step toward me. Then he trots forward and rubs his face against my hand, like he's glad to see *anybody* he knows, even me.

I let out a breath and run my hand over his sleek, bristly body. I could shoo him away, I realize. I could lie and pretend I never saw him. Because if he stays lost, it could be the best thing that's ever happened to me.

But it would also be the meanest thing I've ever done. Because nothing would make Sofía happier than knowing what I know right now.

I lean forward, and he lets me scoop him up. He's a furry little bundle in my arms now—warm and heavy . . . and, I'm not gonna lie, a bit stinky. But I bury my face in his fur and choke back a sob.

Then I scramble to my feet and call as loud as I can, "Sofía! Come quick! I found Oriol!"

17

Sofía crashes through the back door, her face white, her eyes wild.

I run toward her with Oriol in my arms. But when we reach the middle of the yard, she shrinks back like the ground is cracking open between us. She reaches for me, though, breathing fast, making little *come here* motions with her hands. She looks like she's in one of those dreams where you can't move, even though something is chasing you, and the thing you need is just out of reach.

Oriol is warm and real in my arms. His body is vibrating, almost humming. He's never let me hold him before, and I don't want to let go.

But Sofía is shaking as she reaches for him, and I can't make her wait one more second. I step toward her and shift Oriol into her arms.

"*Gatito dulce,*" she murmurs. "*¿Eres tú?*" She holds him out to look him over then cradles him close again. He wraps his tail around her like he's hugging her back. "You found him," she breathes. "You found him. You found him."

"He was chirping under the rainbow feeder," I say. "It worked. It actually *worked*!"

She shakes her head and starts to laugh. The sound rises up like bubbles as I stroke the top of Oriol's head, my chest still warm from where I held him.

But then her laughter changes.

Instead of floating above us, it comes in short bursts, like hiccups. Or like the laugh bubbles are popping and splattering in the air. And then she isn't laughing at all.

She's crying. She's *sobbing*.

She hugs Oriol tight, throws her head back, and wails like I've never seen.

I pull my hand back. I don't know what to do. I can't decide if I should hug her or shake her or take Oriol away. So I drop my arms and just watch her cry, my chest heaving, my stomach hurting.

I don't get it! I've done everything I can think of for her. And Oriol is *home*. He's safe like she wanted. She should be overjoyed! But she's the saddest I've ever seen her instead. "Oriol's here," I say. "We finally found him. Why aren't you happy?"

She squeezes her eyes shut. "Because I'm leaving."

My heart beats in my throat. "But you *like* California. You said it was like home."

"But this is home too," she cries.

Hope flames in my heart. She wants to stay! I wished for it on her candle, in the Magic Mist, by crossing my fingers. And it's coming true! But when I jump for joy, Oriol startles in Sofía's arms. He narrows his eyes at me, like I can't be trusted.

I reach toward him again, slowly. I wonder if he has more than one home after all, like Eli said. I doubt it. Not with how skinny and dirty he looks.

But does Sofía?

I look at the tears streaming down the sides of her face and dripping from her chin. She *does* have another home, I realize. She's part of a flock in California—part of a family that laughs and plays and makes music together. I think that makes her happy.

And I want her to be happy. Even more than I want her to stay.

I stroke Oriol under the chin. He relaxes and presses his face into my hand. Then I take a big breath, look her in the eye, and say, "You love it there, Sofía."

"But there are earthquakes," she wails.

"Not usually big ones."

"And there's no snow," she says. "I'll never go sledding."

"You won't need to go sledding. You can surf."

Sofía looks right at me, her lip trembling. "But you won't be there."

Tears gather in my throat. For a minute, they take up all the room I need for words. Then I swallow them down and loop my pinky finger through her bracelet. "I'll be here," I say.

Sofía takes a shuddery breath, her shoulders slumping. I put my arm around her. She rests her head on my shoulder and hugs Oriol tighter. We watch the sun going down through the trees until her tears stop and her breathing slows. The shadows reach out to kiss our toes as the last golden light slips across the yard.

And I think maybe *this* is what a good friend does. She stands nearby for as long as she can. She holds her friend close—maybe even holds her up—until it's time to let go.

It's almost time now.

But not yet.

We've missed too much already—times we were apart, times we were fighting, even times we didn't play together because we thought we always could.

We're not missing this.

"Come on," I say, standing up straighter. "We're wasting our sleepover."

Sofía sighs. "Our last one."

"Our *best* one," I say.

She lifts her head. "What should we do?"

"Whatever you want. We could build a fort and eat our favorite snacks and make something beautiful. Let's just make this a sleepover we'll never forget."

She laughs—not bubbles yet, but fizz maybe.

"But first," I say, "can we finish our game? It's still your turn to be It."

"Okay." She buries her face in Oriol's fur and starts to count. "One . . . two . . ."

For a moment, I look into those yellow cat eyes. Then I take off running across the yard. But before I slip under the tarp, I check again. Oriol is still watching, his tail swishing, his eyes somehow getting brighter in the fading light. He chirps at me. *"Ack-ack-ack!"*

I duck under the tarp and grin. Because this time, I *want* him to give me away. I want him to lead Sofía right to me.

She might be leaving, but I want her to know where to find me.

Always.

18

I wake up in my sleeping bag on Sofía's floor.

Light is filtering through the windows. It's brighter without the curtains, but it's still that wimpy light that comes before the sun is up.

I stare at a crack in the ceiling. Huh. I never noticed it before. I wonder what else I've missed in all the years I've been coming here.

I'm not missing anything now. Sofía is in her sleeping bag next to me, Oriol curled up at her side. Her cheeks always turn pink when she sleeps. It makes her look younger, like she's in kindergarten again. She looks like she did when we met. I match my breathing to hers and soak it all in—the crack above me, the silver light all around, my best friend by my side.

When I finally sit up, Oriol stretches out his paws and arches his back. Last night, Sofía poured him a big bowl of cat food that smelled like sawdust and tuna. He attacked it like he hadn't eaten in days. After that, she pulled him into her lap to brush him. She kept at it, long into the night. Even after her Mom made us turn out the light, I could hear Oriol purring while Sofía murmured to him in Spanish and worked the knots out of his fur.

He gives a wide-mouthed yawn now. His ears twitch as I roll up my sleeping bag, slip into my sneakers, and pull my rainbow hoodie over my pajamas. Before I creep out the door, Oriol walks himself around in a circle and nestles back down.

Maybe he's not so bad after all. And if Sofía has to go away, I'm glad she's not going alone. A teeny tiny part of me might even miss him.

Dumb cat.

I take one last look at those yellow eyes and tiptoe out of the room.

The birds are tweeting loudly as I walk home. Everywhere I look, I see cardinals, finches, and chickadees in the trees and hopping along the grass. They're even perched on my bird feeders! All those milk jugs we left on doorsteps are hanging from branches and porch ceilings.

I stretch out my arms and fly past them all. I have to get ready. I'm giving Sofía the best send-off in the world. It'll be colorful and exciting—like a rocket taking off or fireworks exploding in the sky. I want her to remember it forever.

To remember *me* forever.

But my workshop is empty, so when I get home, I rummage for other supplies. I drape toilet paper over our bushes like streamers. I borrow colorful flags from our neighbor's yard and poke them all along the curb. They say weird things like *gas* and *water*, but they sure look festive flickering in the breeze. I even find three different colors of spray paint in the garage. I'm just finishing spraying *Good luck, Sofía!* on the grass when Dad gets back from his run.

He doesn't say a word. He just stands there rubbing the back of his neck. Finally, he blows out a breath and says, "I think I'll go let Mom know how hard you've been working."

So it must look *awesome.*

When it's almost time, I pace the sidewalk until Sofía's family pulls up. They're like a mini parade with the moving van rattling and their car trailing behind. Sofía tumbles out of the back seat and squeals at my decorations. She twirls and laughs her bubble laugh until my smile is so wide it hurts.

Our parents are giving one another hugs when Eli comes running up with his book. Sofía reaches into the car, pulls out the cat carrier, and holds it up to show him.

He stops short. "No way."

She beams. "He came back, just like you said."

"He also said Oriol might *not* come back," I remind her.

Eli shrugs. "It's not my fault I know so much about cats."

"You don't know *that* much," I say.

"I do too!" He puffs out his chest. "Did you know adult cats only meow to talk to people? And that they can *taste* how things *smell*?"

Sofía laughs and sets the carrier on the sidewalk. The three of us gather around it and peer in through the little wire door.

"I know something else, too," Eli says mysteriously. "Something you don't."

"What?" she asks.

Eli opens his book to a page of white cats with patches of orange and black. "Oriol is a calico," he says, his eyes gleaming.

"What's that?" I say.

"It's a cat with colored spots like this."

"So?"

"So calico cats . . ." He leans in close. "They're female."

Sofía and I stare at him. "But Oriol isn't," I say.

"Yes, he is." Eli laughs. "*She* is."

Sofía claps a hand over her mouth.

"But the vet would have told them," I stammer.

She shakes her head, eyes wide. "My mom is

the one who takes him for checkups. But if the vet only speaks English—"

I burst out laughing and peer into the cat carrier. "You sneaky little devil!"

"Is that why he ran away?" Sofía asks. "Because I didn't know? Do you think it hurt his feelings?"

"*Her* feelings," Eli says.

She groans.

"No way," I say. "I bet there's lots you don't know about Oriol, like what she does when she's not with you." I shrug. "Now you know a little more."

Sofía's dad comes over and rests a hand on her shoulder. "Time to go, Sofía *mía*."

She bites her lip and nods. Eli sticks his finger into the cage door for one last pet. When it's my turn, Oriol leans into my finger like the two of us are old friends. Then Sofía's dad lifts the carrier into the car.

"Send us pictures of the birds out there," Eli says as we get to our feet.

"I will," Sofía says. "Send pictures of your new rabbit."

Eli shifts from one foot to the other. "Here." He holds out his cat book.

She draws back a little. "I can't break up the set."

"You're already doing that," he says.

She takes it and runs her fingers gently over the cover. Then she reaches into the back seat and hands him her bird book. "The birds are different there anyway," she says quietly.

He toes the sidewalk. "I bet they're just as nice."

For a moment, they both stand blinking at their new books. Then she leans over and gives him a quick kiss on the cheek. Eli's ears go pink.

"Come here, Rosie Posey," Sofía says, opening her arms to my sister. Rosie drops Pink Pony and hurtles forward. Sofía lifts her off the ground and twirls her until she squeals. When she's back on her feet, Rosie hugs her tight around the stomach for a long time.

Then Sofía lets go and turns to me.

The quicksand fills up my stomach, sucking down all the good, happy feelings.

No. I can do this. I *will* do this. For her.

I run to the front stoop and bring her the big plastic jar that I filled with Rainbow Pops. "I hope it's enough color to last until California."

She smiles and turns it over in her hands. When the cereal tumbles inside, the jar looks like a kaleidoscope. She sets it in the back seat and hands me a roll of paper. "This is for you."

I open it up. It's an explosion of dry paint and handprints—yellow and orange, purple and red. It's half of our poster, I realize, the one I thought she didn't want.

"Now we both have one," she says, "like our bracelets. And next time we see each other, we can add new handprints."

"When will that be?"

Her smile falters. "Maybe next summer?"

My mouth goes dry. That's more than a year from now. Her hands could be twice as big by then. She might be six feet tall with hair down to her ankles. She'll probably have a whole clowder of cats.

I lay the paper gently in the grass and grab her hand. "Come on." I lead her around to the backyard then open my arms and turn a slow circle. "Pick one."

She gazes at all the milk jugs, swaying and spinning in the breeze. "Which one?"

I hesitate. A good friend would point out the bird feeder she'd like best, not the scrappy, lopsided one I want her to have. So I point to a jug that's covered with dainty little hearts and flowers. "That one's the prettiest."

She nods. Then she walks over to the garden, to the feeder with crooked stripes of tape. "This is the one that brought Oriol home, right?"

My heart does a squeeze. "It's not very pretty."

"But it's the most colorful." She smiles. "It's the one that reminds me of you."

Tears swell in my throat. I hide my face as I

untie the feeder. When I turn back around, Sofía's lip is starting to quiver.

No. We're *not* getting sad now.

I hand her the feeder, my mind racing. There must be something I can do to make her happy again—some way to wrap her up in color and cheer. But my supplies are gone. I have nothing to give her. I hug myself, my heart aching.

Then I pull my hoodie off over my head. "Take this too."

She takes a step back. "But it's your favorite."

"You're my favorite." I tug it over her head until it gets stuck then keep yanking at it while she giggles and squeals. When she finally finds the armholes, she pulls it down to her waist and flips back the hood. "Just think of me when you wear it," I say.

She smiles her brightest, most sun-shiny smile. "I'd think of you anyway."

I grin. "Race you to the car."

We run around the house, laughing and elbowing each other out of the way. We slap the side of the car at the same time and stand there panting and beaming until her dad opens the door. "I almost forgot," Sofía says, reaching inside. She turns and hands me a jug. "We finished our milk this morning."

I blink at it. "I don't have a collection anymore."

"You will." She gives me a big hug and climbs into the car.

Then she's riding away at the back of her own personal parade, leaning out the window and blowing kisses, looking like an explosion of color in my tie-dyed hoodie. I run after her with Eli and Rosie, all of us shouting and waving until she rides over a hill and disappears.

I slow down then, staring at the empty place where Sofía was.

And suddenly, I can't fight the quicksand anymore. It pulls me to the sidewalk. I sink down and wrap my arms around myself. Eli and Rosie drop to their knees and hug me from either side. Then Mom and Dad are wrapping us up from behind, and everyone is holding me up while the hurt blasts through me.

But even as I slump there, gasping for air, I feel my family all around and know in some happy scrap of my heart that Sofía is flying toward her own flock now.

And I know I'm a good friend after all.

Because I let her go. Because I sent her off smiling, her kitty by her side, bright and happy and full of hope.

19

I don't think I'll ever cry again.

Someday I'll stub my toe or bite my tongue, and I'll shout and pound my fists, but no tears will come, because I used them all up today.

My eyes are still puffy as I sit in the tractor tire out back. I scoop dry sand into Sofía's milk jug and dump it out. Fill it. Empty it. Fill and empty, over and over, all afternoon. Rosie is picking dandelions nearby, like she's keeping an eye on me. I catch Mom and Dad spying on me from the kitchen window too. They did the same thing after I had my first seizure. It was like they were afraid I might explode any second.

But you need energy to explode. You need something bursting inside you. And I feel the opposite of that.

I feel empty.

I want to hold on to how happy I was for Sofía to join her flock. But my happiness feels

wispy, like clouds breezing past the solid mountains of sadness inside me.

"Meena?" Rosie is standing over my shoulder
now.

"What."

"Can we plant something in the Magic Garden?"

I scoop more sand into the jug. "Not now."

"But it's Sunday."

"There's nothing to plant."

She dangles her baggie of chicken feed in front
of me. "Yes, there is."

"That probably won't even grow anything."

"But what if it does?" When I look up, her
brown eyes are twinkling.

I don't know what to tell her. I can't think of
anything the chicken feed could turn into. "It won't
work," I say dully. "Tomorrow is May. The garden
will lose its magic."

"But today is still April. Please?"

I turn the jug over and watch sand pour out
in a long, even stream. "We shouldn't get our hopes
up, Rosie."

She gives my shoulder a kiss. "I think we should."

She skips across the yard then. I hear her singing her little song while she digs in the garden. She
sprinkles chicken feed into the ground and bends
down to cover it up.

And I do feel something building inside me now.

I want to yell across the yard and warn her: *You can't keep everything!* Magic ends. Treasures disappear. Friends fly far, far away. You can't stop it. Rosie needs to know that.

But when she brushes the dirt off her knees, I know I won't be the one to tell her. Not today. I toss my jug aside.

She'll find out soon enough.

Rosie is still asleep on Monday morning when I put on my necklace and slip past her.

I barely recognize my workshop now. Our kindergarten painting is on the wall where I hung it yesterday—half of it, anyway. But the colorful handprints look too cheerful in the empty room. The floor is bare except for streaks of marker staining the carpet. Mom did save a few things that I guess she knew were special: my valentine box, my supersuit, the jar of can tabs Sofía gave me. The rest is crayons and markers, glue and scissors—the stuff I make stuff *with*, not what I make it *from*.

I tiptoe to the window and breathe Magic Mist on the glass. There are so many things I want back—the igloo, my treasures, Sofía. But I think the Mist gets offended if you wish for something that can't come true. So I just stare at the circle of fog until it disappears, holding my wishes inside.

At breakfast, I push Rainbow Pops around

my bowl. Everyone is quiet, watching me. "Can we check the garden?" Rosie asks.

But I know there's nothing to find, so I just say, "Later."

A phone pings on the counter. Dad checks the screen as I swallow my pill. "Sofía's dad says they made it to Colorado."

I can't picture Colorado. In my mind, it's just a plain blue rectangle in the middle of the reading rug.

But Sofía isn't on the rug when I get to school. She isn't anywhere I look—on the playground or in her desk, in the slide or sitting across from me at lunch. The only time I feel like she's close is at my cubby at the end of the day. While I'm packing up, I can almost hear her asking, *Did you remember your spelling list?*

It figures she'd be talking about homework.

"Meena?" I look up and see Mrs. D walking toward me as the hallway clears. She stops and opens her mouth, but nothing comes out. Finally, she gives me sad eyes and says, "I'm so sorry about Sofía."

I look at my feet.

She gives the top of my arm a squeeze. "I know how hard it is to lose someone."

"She isn't lost," I say. "She's in Colorado."

Mrs. D hesitates. "To miss someone, then. And I know how close you were. I know the two of you were like this." She holds up a hand, her fingers crossed.

I cross my own fingers and clench my hands into fists. But this time, I'm not telling a lie or making a wish. I'm holding tight to something that's already gone.

Mrs. D gives me a kind smile. It's the same smile she gave Sofía when we told her Oriol was lost. "But look on the bright side," she says.

"Mrs. D?"

She raises her eyebrows at me.

"I can't look at any bright sides right now."

She blinks fast. "Okay. But if you need anything . . . anything at all . . ."

I give a quick nod and hurry down the hall.

I'm still crossing my fingers when I get to the bike rack. I stare at the empty space for a minute before I remember that I didn't bring my wagon today. I start walking, but I don't bother to look for interesting trash. Mom doesn't want me dragging that stuff home anyway.

I do notice the milk jugs, though. They're hanging in almost every yard I pass. It makes my heart ache to see our igloo, broken apart and scattered like that. One of the jugs is missing too. The rainbow feeder I gave to Sofía is moving farther away every minute. It won't stop until it reaches that silly ocean she was so excited about.

And suddenly, I don't want to go home to my empty workshop or a yard full of bird feeders reminding me of everything I lost. So I dig out my walkie-talkie.

"Mom?" I don't call her *Mama Zee*. She doesn't use her call handle anyway.

"What's up, honey?" she answers.

My shoulders sag. *Big Zee*, I think. "Nothing. I'm just going to Eli's."

"Okay. Let me know when you're coming home."

I think of all the things I could answer. *Roger. Ten-four. I read you loud and clear.* But I don't say any of them, and I don't sign off.

I just stuff the walkie-talkie back into my bag.

Aunt Kathy lets me in. Red curls are coming loose from her ponytail, and she's still in her scrubs from work. "Hey, sweetheart," she says. "He's in his room."

Eli is doing after-school rounds with his animals. I spot Sofía's bird book on his shelf, smack in the middle of his *All About Animals* books, even though it doesn't match. I check the whiteboard to see if there's something I can do. I don't want to pet anything, and I'm not scooping poop, but he hasn't fed Lizzy yet, so I grab the fish food.

But when I go to sprinkle it over the water, I see that Lizzy isn't in her tank. The bubbler is bubbling, and fake seaweed is swaying at the bottom of the aquarium like there's a breeze . . . but no Lizzy. I glance at Eli. "Did she—?"

His eyes flick to me and away again. "Yesterday."

I cringe. "I guess cleaning the tank didn't help."

He closes the top of his guinea pig cage with a frown. "She was almost six," he says. "That's really old for a betta fish."

I set down the fish food and gaze into the water. Eli comes to stand next to me. He looks at the empty tank for a minute then wipes his eyes on the back of his sleeve.

Hang on. Is he *crying*?

I watch him smear away tears with the heel of his hand. I just lost my best friend, and he's crying over a *fish*? "What are you so sad about?" I ask. "Can't you get a new fish for, like, five bucks?"

He glares at me. "A new fish wouldn't be Lizzy."

"Oh." I shrink back. "Sorry, it's just . . ." I rub the back of my neck. "Well, you have so many pets. I thought you were used to this part."

"I mean, I'm not *surprised*, but I'm still sad."

"Then why do you have all these animals when they're just gonna . . ." I stop.

He blinks at me. "Because it's not all like this. I get to play with them and take care of them and spend time with them." He shrugs. "It's still worth it, even if I can't keep them forever."

I look back at the empty water. How could it be worth it? If he didn't love that dumb fish so much, he wouldn't feel so bad about losing her.

And if I'd never met Sofía, I wouldn't be missing her now.

But I do miss her. So much. Already. Maybe I always will.

I cross my fingers and wish I could stop. I wish I could forget I ever knew her. I'd do it, if it would save me from hurting now.

But then I remember making our painting together. I think of all those recesses we huddled in the slide. I picture her passing me can tabs across the lunch table, her eyes shining.

I uncross my fingers. I wouldn't give up any of those things, I realize. Not a single one. But if I could do our friendship all over again, I would change one thing.

I'd do it better.

I'd meet her sooner, play with her longer, and give her more turns, right from the start. I'd pay closer attention to the things she cared about. I wouldn't waste days being mad, and I'd never save projects for *someday*.

I'd be a good friend at the beginning and all the way through, like Eli is to his pets.

I glance at the whiteboard, at all those checkmarks next to all those animals. Then I reach over and take hold of his sleeve. "Lizzy was lucky to have you," I say.

He lifts his other hand and touches a finger to her tank. "I was lucky to have her, too."

For a minute we stand like that. Tiny air bubbles sparkle in the water, making rainbow colors in the light. "Are you still getting another rabbit?" I ask finally.

Eli brightens a little. "We put the hutch together yesterday. Wanna see?"

I follow him out to the back porch. At first, seeing the place where the igloo *isn't* takes my breath away. The new hutch is nestled in our corner now, filling up the space where our club used to meet.

But it's nothing like our clubhouse. It's clean and pretty and new. It looks like a gingerbread house with a pointy roof, a fake chimney, and double doors that open to a balcony. There's even a ramp that leads to a play yard, surrounded by a tiny picket fence.

I start to laugh. "It's so fancy! Vernon's really moving up in the world."

Eli beams. "Do you like it?"

"Yeah. But it's big enough for *ten* rabbits. What's he gonna do with all that space?"

"What do you think?" Eli grins. "He'll make a new friend."

20

On my walk home, I scan the ground for interesting trash. I don't find any doll heads or sunglass lenses or broken combs. But I will. Eventually. If I keep looking, I know I'll find something amazing.

The garage door is open when I get home. Mom must have dropped off our donations, because the boxes are gone. It feels big and bare in here now. Empty storage containers are stacked in the corner. I wander over and gaze into the one on top, thinking of all the toys and books and clothes I'll never see again. I run my hands along the rim, and my stomach squeezes a little.

Then all of a sudden, I get an Inspiration.

I drop my backpack, pull the bins apart, and start dragging them across the floor. I line them up under the workbench, side by side. Then I stand back to take a look. This is a good spot. The bins are out of the way here but easy to get to.

Just then, the walkie-talkie crackles in my

backpack. I hear Mom's voice. It sounds muffled, like she's talking underwater. "Mama Zee to Big Zee. All units, report. Repeat, all units, report, over."

Hang on. Did she just use my call handle? And *hers*?

I dig the walkie-talkie out of my bag. "Big Zee here. I read you loud and clear, Mama Zee. Go ahead, over."

"What's your ten-forty, over?"

I stare at the speaker. "Come again? Over."

"Shoot, I mean . . . Stand by." There's a pause, like she's looking something up. "Your ten-*twenty*," she says after a minute. "What's that, over?"

I grin. "I'm in the garage, over."

The side door opens and Mom peeks in. She holds the walkie-talkie to her mouth again. "Copy that, Big Zee. This is Mama Zee, over and out." She hooks the handset onto her pants.

"Nice job," I say.

She shrugs, looking a little shy. "I figured I'd get hip to the lingo."

"Hip to the what?"

"I thought it was time I learned to speak your language." She looks around. "What are you doing out here?"

I glance at the bins. "Making a new storage area."

Her shoulders stiffen. She looks past me and crosses to the workbench.

I hurry after her. "I know what you're going to say. I can't keep everything. And I won't. But I need to keep *some* things. Because I can't make something out of nothing."

She rubs her forehead. Her eyes flick to me, then back to the bins. "What are you planning to make?"

I thrust my chin out. "I don't know. But you said to make space for things I care about and things I haven't thought of yet. That's why I collect trash. Because I care about it. And because I use it to make things I haven't thought of yet."

I hold my breath, waiting. It seems like Mom stands there for a long time before she finally says, "Okay."

I step back. "Okay?"

She lets out a breath. "You and I are very different, Meena. I like my space. You like your stuff." She smiles at me. "But maybe you can have too much of either one."

I perk up. "Does that mean—?"

"You have to wash everything you keep," she says, pointing at me. "And when the bins are full, they're full. No bringing home more until you make room. Deal?" She holds out her hand.

I pump it up and down. "Deal!"

Her face seems to cloud over then. "I never would have gotten rid of everything if I'd known Sofía was leaving," she says.

"Really?"

"I mean, I would have thrown away the rotting garbage, but . . ." She tucks my hair behind my ear. "I didn't know so many things would be changing for you at once. I'm sorry."

"I'm sorry too." I scuff my foot against the cement. "I shouldn't have lied. And I should have cleaned up when you told me to." I crinkle my nose. "And I'm sorry about the smell."

She chuckles. "Do over?"

I nod. "Do over."

I turn back to my new storage bins. Somehow, the sight of all that empty space doesn't bother me the way it used to. It makes me feel peaceful. And hopeful. Like something new is coming.

I'll start another collection, like Sofía said. Because if you pay attention, you see beautiful things everywhere, even in places you never expect. In birds. In cats. In faraway places you've never been to.

Maybe someday you'll visit.

Now what should I put in here first?

"My jug," I say with a start. "Where's my jug?"

"What jug?" Mom asks.

"The one Sofía gave me."

"Oh . . . You had it in the sandbox."

"Right! Thanks, Mom!" I give her a quick hug and dash outside.

Rosie is sitting in the tractor tire, starting a new castle. My jug is still in the grass where I tossed it yesterday. I turn it over and dump out the last of the sand.

"What's that for?" Rosie asks.

"Come and see."

She follows me into the garage and watches me drop my very first jug into the bin. It makes a nice thump as it lands. "What are you saving it for?" she asks.

"I don't know yet."

But whatever it is, I'll be ready.

Suddenly, Rosie lets out a little gasp. "We have to check the garden."

Oh, no. The chicken feed!

She runs for the door.

"Rosie, wait," I cry. "Let's check it later!"

"Come on," she calls over her shoulder.

I run after her, my mind racing. "It needs more time," I shout. "It needs more sun!"

But she keeps running, and I can't catch her.

What will I tell her? I can't let her down. And the magic makes her happy, even though it's a lie. Maybe it won't last forever. But it can't end *now*. She's too little. And I wasn't supposed to do anything mean!

But she's at the edge of the garden already, reaching for something pink.

I stop short. I stand there, blinking, then take the last few steps until I'm close enough to see something on the wooden skewers, little shapes that look like—

Marshmallow chicks?

I gasp. "Where did those come from?"

Rosie claps her hands and squeals. "I told you we could grow chickens!"

I rub my eyes and look again. The candy chicks are still there, the pink sugar sparkling in the sun. "It really *is* a magic garden," I whisper. It must be! Where else would they come from?

Rosie smiles up at me as I slide a marshmallow bird off the stick. It's a little stale on the outside, but it still squishes. "Do you know what this means?" I cup my hands around it like it's a real baby bird. "We can probably grow anything we want! Cakes, cookies, ice cream—"

Rosie starts to giggle. She covers her mouth with both hands.

"What's so funny?" I ask.

She throws back her head and roars with laughter. Then she slaps her thighs, flings out her arms, and yells, "April Fools'!"

Wait a second.

I stare at the pink chickens, all lined up in a

row. Then I look back at Rosie. "*You* did this?"

She beams at me.

"But how—" I take a step back, my eyes wide. "Rosalyn Zee, you *knew*?"

"Not right away," she says with a shrug.

"When?"

And I'm not sure, but I'm almost positive she rolls her eyes before she says, "The donuts should have had sprinkles."

"Then why did you go along with it?"

She tilts her head at me. "Because it made you happy."

I smack my forehead.

"And because next year," she says, her eyes sparkling, "we can plant pennies and grow dollar bills!"

I snort. "Where would we get the money?"

"From Mom and Dad."

"But don't they know that you *know*? About the Magic Garden? Didn't they give you the marshmallow chicks?"

"No." Rosie gives me a sly grin. "Eli did."

My jaw drops open. Then I burst out laughing. "Atta girl," I say, mussing her hair.

And it turns out I'm kind of relieved that I don't have to keep lying to her, even if it *is* just for fun. But the prank doesn't have to end. It just has to change.

And Rosie will be a great partner.

My brain starts sparking with ideas of things we could grow next year in our so-called Magic Garden. Maybe we'll even plant cat food and get our own kitten!

Whoa. I give myself a shake. Where did *that* idea come from?

"Hey, you two!"

Mom and Dad are strolling across the yard toward us. Dad is talking on his phone, and when they get close, I hear him say, "She'd love that. Just a sec, I'll put her on."

He holds it out to me.

"Who is it?" I ask.

He smiles. "Who do you think?"

I glance at Rosie, then put the phone to my ear. "This is Big Zee, over."

"Meena!" I hear laughter, like bubbles rising into the air.

I gasp. "Sofía? Where are you?"

"Mom says we're almost through Nevada," she says. "It's like summer here, Meena! I already changed into my sandals."

I whirl around, my heart swelling inside me.

"I can see the mountains too," she says. "They're brown and really far away, but they're so pretty!"

I smile. "Any trees fall on you yet?"

Sofía laughs again. "Not yet, but I'll watch out. What are you doing?"

"Just picking marshmallows. Did you eat all the Rainbow Pops?"

"No, I'm making them last. I gave some to Oriol, but they made her puke. I'll send you pictures."

"Of Oriol's puke?"

"Of the drive, silly. And I'll call when we get there. Oh, and we missed our club yesterday, but I found my three things now! Tell Eli I've already seen hawks and roadrunners and even some quails. I'll talk to you soon, okay?"

"Okay, talk to you soon!" I end the call and lower the phone. Rosie is showing Mom and Dad the garden. She hands them each a marshmallow chick. When she sees me watching, she gives me a great big wink.

I wink back, Sofía's voice humming in my head.

She'll call when she gets there. I'll talk to her soon.

And we still have a club—with a new location opening soon in California!

I look down at the rainbow-colored friendship bracelet around my wrist. Sofía isn't *gone*, I realize. I haven't lost her. Not like I've been thinking.

She's out there somewhere, driving through Nevada. I've never been there before, but I know it's orange on the reading rug and shaped like an upside-down house. And I know it has brown mountains and birds that look like cartoon pears when they run.

Sofía is there right now, on her way to people she loves.

But she loves me, too. And if she *is* a sparrow, maybe I can still be part of her flock.

I cross my fingers, turn a slow circle, and gaze at all those milk jugs hanging from the trees. Our igloo. Our beat-up, crooked little igloo.

It's not gone either. It's just different now.

But it's still strong and flexible. It's swaying and spinning in the breeze, letting the birds know they're home.

Acknowledgments

I wrote this story during the first wave of the COVID-19 pandemic. Sticking to a writing routine amid the losses and uncertainty of 2020 is one of the hardest things I've ever done. During that tumultuous time, however, the whole team at Simon & Schuster Books for Young Readers was unfailingly professional and kind. I am especially grateful to senior editor Krista Vitola and associate editor Catherine Laudone for championing this series at every turn. Thanks to designer Tom Daly and illustrator Mina Price for creating the look and feel of the book. I also owe a debt of gratitude to expert readers Crystal Velasquez and Jan De la Rosa for late-stage corrections and insights. As always, special thanks to my agent, the ever-steady-at-the-wheel Emily Mitchell.

I am grateful for a crew of family and friends who faithfully cheer me on, even when the world seems upside down. The women of Red Barn found a way to celebrate my second book when in-person events were cancelled. Rick Rupprecht and Jenny Bos answered questions outside my expertise. J. Mercer gave important feedback when I was sure

I'd lost my way. Carolyn Manternach and Erika Edberg Manternach caught mistakes the rest of us missed, as usual.

In the end, though, I couldn't have finished this book without the love and support of my husband and kids. Amelia and Mara, you left me alone when my door was closed, gave me hugs when I came up for air, and read the finished story out loud so I could see what made you laugh and cry. (You also set me straight about the fish.) And Brian, Meena might be the main character of this story, but you are its unsung hero. When everything felt overwhelming and impossible, you stopped at nothing to make our lives work. Thank you, thank you, my love.

Finally, to my readers: I hope you love this book as much as I do! Writing it was a Hard Thing, but I did it for you.